Although Adelle was foreign to her own anger, she and Rose had lived together so long that she allowed herself to get angry in front of Rose. It was not the kind of anger most would notice. Adelle would stare at Rose for a while, usually playing with a part of her own face or arm, and then say something much too loudly, such as "Did you water the plants today?"

Rose knew, when Adelle asked such things, that the answer was not important. The plants were not important. Rose could make any reply, and Adelle would leap out of her chair, almost knocking it backwards in her haste, and scream as though an outrage of great proportions had just been committed. "NEVER MIND. I'll do it, just like I do everything else around here." Then she would water every plant unlucky enough to be in sight, dousing them with water as though to wash away a lifetime of sins.

Sometimes Rose thought it was funny when Adelle got mad like that. But Adelle had been mad for a week now, and Rose was getting tired. Also, the plants were very wet.

That night, as the paper-thin piece of moon hung in the sky like a bitten off fingernail, Adelle said, so softly that Rose had trouble making out all the words:

"I heard, Rose. I heard about the mammogram. There is quite definitely something there. It's actually larger than it seemed to be on the one which got lost. It's been sent to the surgeon."

The bugs singing in the heat of the night made a sound much like a slowly twirling boat propeller. Rose and Adelle held hands.

ROSE PENSKI

A NOVEL BY ROZ PERRY

ROSE PENSKI

A NOVEL BY ROZ PERRY

The Naiad Press, Inc.
1989

Printed in the United States of America
First Edition

Edited by Katherine V. Forrest
Cover design by Pat Tong and Bonnie Liss
    (Phoenix Graphics)
Typeset by Sandi Stancil

Library of Congress Cataloging-in-Publication Data

Perry, Roz, 1938—
    Rose Penski.

    I. Title.
PS3566.E7163R6 1989   813.54   88-29119
ISBN 0-941483-37-1 (pbk.)

Dedication

To Carole Ashkinaze, for her class, in both meanings of the word.

To the friends who kept my head above water when it was rough and angry, to Joan, to forgot how to swim, to the singing of Mabel Mercer which always soothes me, and to a lovely human being who plays Parcheesi with wild abandon, *will* save the whales, and even does the dishes sometimes.

And, of course to Cyrilly Abels who, years ago, made New York City mine for a day.

Don't worry Millie . . . next one is for you.

About the Author

The author lives on the Gulf of Mexico where brown pelicans rest heavily on the limbs of cedar trees, mullet jump in the marshy wetness of moonlight, and sometimes an entire night goes mad with the sounds of nature. Once a year the author tries to recall which advanced degrees she has, what they have taught her, but then she has a cup of tea and takes a walk on the beach.

ROSE PENSKI

A NOVEL BY ROZ PERRY

While Rose Penski was still in the first half of her single digit years, perhaps as young as five, she fell in love with the little girl around the corner, and she has been doing obscene and bizarre things ever since. The girl was named Faye, and Rose thinks she fell in love because Faye had a nice umbrella with yellow daisies on it. Or, she sometimes muses, perhaps it was not an umbrella at all, but rather a bowl painted with yellow daisies, a bowl with a small turtle living in it. Or maybe the turtle was painted with daisies. However, it is clear, even on muddled days, that it was love and that yellow daisies were somehow involved.

To be in love at age five, Rose Penski recalls, is very intense. She used to cry at the daycare center if she and Faye didn't sit at the same snack table. She would cry long and loud, and the workers would look very nervous and make it a point to always have Faye and Rose at separate tables. They were not even allowed in the same activity groups. Adults do not appreciate the love lives of five-year-olds.

Once they played house, and Faye was the mother. She said, "Rose, you are a very bad girl. I will have to spank you. Bend over." This was the highlight of the actual expression of love between them. It happened in New York City, in an apartment on East Thirteenth Street. Just as the blow was to be felt, Faye's mother came back from shopping at the butcher's and said, "Whatever are you two doing? Clean up this mess."

To this day Rose has a slight resentment of butchers and those who frequent them. Because of this, she often becomes totally vegetarian. However, Rose is an avid cook and reader of countless cookbooks, so it is hard for her to remain a vegetarian for long, or when she is, to remain one totally.

For one so young to have loved so deeply and with such meager results has left scars. Though Rose has had many occupations: teacher, counselor, psychologist, administrator, and the like, she always, when taking a test to determine what to be when she grows up, gets the highest score in "philosopher." There is, Rose Penski often thinks, something obscene and bizarre in the fact that philosopher is even listed as an occupation. Perhaps in the days of yore, when truth was something as sweet as honey in a jar, as simple as a tree branch, it might have been a valid

2

profession. But surely even the makers of tests know that the current world has little use for philosophers. If one must decide the ethical responsibility of a sperm donor who fathers a deformed child, perhaps a philosopher specializing in ethics might be called in. But in truth, what did Plato know of sperm and all that in it is?

Rose does know a person of philosophical bent. He lives in a rather large apartment which Rose has never seen, and he eats peanut butter ice cream when he feels low. He plans to write an important letter to a world leader when he is sure he has clearly thought out what he has to say. Meanwhile, life goes on, and the ice cream melts. He once broke into tears, loneliness standing beside him at the grocery store check-out counter, when the clerk bade him "Have a good day." He cried because it is such a tough job being a philosopher.

With those rather attractive options, philosopher or lover, not looming very large as money-making ventures, Rose Penski busies herself as best she can. She does much more than cook almost vegetarian dishes and tend to the daisies in her garden. Rose Penski has a goal.

Rose wants to read an entire library, each and every book in it. Any library will do. Rose has gotten close a few times, but has always stopped shy of a shelf or two. Still she presses on. She wants to know what other cultures have to teach, what wise persons have learned from living and loving. Rose Penski wants to know so much that her mind will sit silently in the garden of life, content to be blank.

As for love, heaven help us, Rose Penski is still an active player in spite of the Faye fiasco. And, oddly, she still falls in love because of yellow daisies.

* * * * *

Rose and Adelle have lived together for close to eight years. Adelle is a real estate broker. They often have lengthy discussions about Adelle's work, but Rose has never been sure just what it is, exactly, what a broker does. "How," friends often ask, "can you not know *exactly* what it is Adelle does?" They ask this as though it is of great importance that someone know what another person does. These same friends are apt to ask Adelle what Rose is "into" these days. The clear implication is that Adelle ·*does* something, while Rose is *into* things. That might be why Rose Penski never asks Adelle, straight out, what a broker does. On bad days, when things aren't going well, Adelle might snap, "Of course you don't know, but you sure the heck know where the money comes from, don't you?" Adelle rarely swears.

Adelle enjoys her work. She enjoys it so much that she spends long long hours at her office, and still brings home papers to scribble upon. At home she often places phone calls to places such as Nairobi or Pittsburgh. When she does that for long periods of time, Rose sketches things, like Adelle's feet, or the yellow-sharp pencil she bangs up and down on the notepad as she talks.

All in all, it is a pleasant life for Adelle and Rose. They eat well on their almost vegetarian diet, and have many things to discuss besides themselves. Their sex life, though not about to set fires, is comfortably

4

workable. When Adelle was married, years ago when most women did that sort of thing because most women did that sort of thing, her husband once said, "It's been sixty-four days since we've made love." Things were not so bleak on the current home front. Rose Penski is not good at numbers, and can't really remember how long the bad times last. Even if they did last sixty-four days, it wouldn't make a difference. Rose spends her time on other matters.

Adelle's husband had been into insurance, some sort of an odds maker. That might be why he was able to recall so accurately the passage of time between sex. If one were to ask Adelle a number question, such as how long it had been since she and Rose had made love, she would say, one can be certain, "I don't have the pertinent facts at hand right now, but I'd be glad to calculate it if you don't mind waiting."

Rose and Adelle are temporarily living in Fairfax, California, in a small home they've rented for the summer. Behind the house is a small pond. Rose Penski often sits on the bank and knows, with a deep sorrow, that even with her new glasses and days filled with free-floating time, she will never be able to read all the books in the local library. She might, Rose Penski thinks as she slaps at a black fly carving an air castle around her ear, read all the books on one broad subject, such as anthropology. She is always saddened, as she travels, that she has never yet managed to read an entire library, even small ones such as this one.

As Adelle leaves for work each morning, kicking up the greyed dust which is a Northern California summer, she says, "I'll be in the computer room if you want me. They can ring you through." Rose Penski won't call. It is just too hard to compete with a computer. Adelle will spend the day pushing buttons to describe homes on hillsides, homes in valleys, homes on waterfronts. She won't even visit many of the homes, just read about them, price them, and write about them in the green-lit computer room.

Adelle might have cancer. They have come from their home far up the coast so that they can relax by the pond, on the hillside, and have tests done in San Francisco. Adelle is using a branch office in the city to keep from falling behind in her work.

Rose bites into a peach and tastes the bitter soft taste of a brown spot. She spits it out, wondering if cancer in a human is like such a spot. Fish swim in the polluted waters of the pond, jumping up to guzzle flies, and birds swoop down for a quick lunch.

* * * * *

When Rose Penski was seven, love touched her life again, and she learned that it is easier to love than to be loved. And thus it is that philosophers are born.

In Rose's first grade class, there was a poor boy. Rose and the other students knew he was poor because at the start of each school session he wore his cousin's hand-me-down clothes. His cousin was in the same class, and was named Harold. The poor cousin was named Billy. Billy fell in love with Rose Penski, would follow her into the cloakroom at the start of the day and say, in what Rose felt to be a most sinister manner, "I want you to K.I.S.S. me."

Now, in the days of long ago and youth, long

before fluorescent lighting, cloakrooms were dark. They were places of sin. And in the days before *Sesame Street,* people didn't talk by spelling. So the "K.I.S.S. me" was very scary.

One fog-draped day, while Rose was hanging up her jacket and dreading Billy's voice, Peter Reese came in. He didn't say a word to Rose, just hung up his jacket next to her sweater. His jacket was a plaid one made of scratchy wool. It was blue and white and black. It hung there, next to Rose's, and it seemed to her like a light, a beacon. Peter seemed unaware of the fact that he was a savior, a saint, a knight in shining armor. His jacket next to Rose Penski's kept Billy away, and a pleasant safety returned to the cloakroom. Rose loved Peter all through grade school. And although Billy maintained his lustful yearnings towards Rose, he kept his distance. One of the first things Rose bought for herself as an adult was a lumber jacket of blue, white and black plaid. It was too itchy to wear very often. Years later she read in a newspaper somewhere that Peter had done something fine, had won a coveted award. It pleased her greatly.

Having loved twice and been loved once by the age of seven, Rose Penski was well versed in the subject, though the memory of yellow daisies and the memory of the cloakroom were different, and she felt herself somewhat of an Ann Landers. It angered her slightly that it was so much easier for Billy to whisper, "K.I.S.S. me," than it was for her to sit next to Faye. Such, however, was life.

If one were to ask Adelle about love she would probably say, "I don't know. I never have time for such things." She would say that in a manner which mostly asked you to believe was lying. Of course Adelle must have loved. Maybe she is loathe to say because she was, herself, a cloakroom marauder. These things follow us around forever.

* * * * *

Rose decided to leave Adelle during their stay in Fairfax. It was a hot dry night, with bugs jumping against the window panes trying to eat the light. One could almost hear the dust settling down in the darkness outside, gaining strength for tomorrow's onslaught. Frogs made deep clicking-like croaks, and the moon appeared to be swimming in the black water of the pond. Adelle had wiped off all the counter tops. She had, as a matter of fact, done it several times.

Dressed only in a greying nylon nightgown, one left over from her married days so long ago, she scrubbed away at the years of grime which had collected that day. Wiping the sweat from her brow, and pushing a stray blonde wisp of hair behind her ear, she said in a tone of total sorrow, "I guess I'll lock up."

Rose, who had started her anthropology reading with male bonding, tossed aside Lionel Tiger (and well she should have) and braced herself for trouble. "I've done it. The doors are all locked. The windows are sealed tight. The flue is secure. The door chains are anchored firm." Adelle put down her cleaning rag and looked heavenward, though all that lent was a view of the kitchen ceiling tiles which leaked a bit and had orange stains from the hard water. She clutched her forehead. "I'd better check, just to make sure."

Now any fool, even a philosopher, could tell that this meant Rose's door-locking skills were in question. "I said I did it."

Adelle picked up the cleaning rag, folded it once, and put it back under the sink. She gave Rose Penski a loving look. "I'll just double check."

Rose Penski, for reasons known only to the imp of love, said to herself, "If she so much as touches a door, we are through." Wise persons who think these things through, those who follow all the rules in the *Egyptian Book of the Dead* and eat a well-balanced diet, might think this odd of Rose. But those who follow the adventures of lovers in the tabloids of the universe will know. They will say to themselves with a knowing heart, "Of course. If Adelle checks the doors, love will lie in a dead heap just beyond the doorknob." Adelle checked.

The doors, of course, had been secure. The relationship was not. So many years of uphill plodding: the times in bed, at breakfast, walking, talking. The days, nay, weeks, when Rose was into Persian cooking and the whole house smelled of dill. The time when she was into making her own yeast, and the hose stank of beer for a month. The times Adelle brought home pounds of computer printouts and sat in bed, bits of potato salad clinging to her lips as she angrily zapped a number here, a notation there. All these memories gone. And why? Because Adelle had to check the locks.

The checking done, they went to bed with double security, and in a way they knew the sunrise would be different. Rose Penski dreamed, as they slept far apart on the small double bed, a skill only practiced dodgers of love have mastered, of a heavy wool jacket. She was wearing it, chasing some piece of something, some bit of memory, down a foggy street. Winds from a salty bay splashed against her brow, but the jacket kept her warm and safe. Even in her fitful sleep, while taking care not to so much as brush her lover with warmth, Rose Penski could feel Adelle dreaming.

As usual, Adelle ate breakfast in her nylon slip tucked, for modesty's sake, into the rim of her bra, so that her stomach was covered but her knees peaked out a good foot beneath the hemline. Rose told Adelle her dream, asking what she had dreamt. "Nothing that I recall." Adelle, still in a bad mood, ate only three dried prunes, a cup of black coffee, and a stale sweet roll which Rose had been saving to feed the birds. She ignored the breakfast Rose had waiting.

Rose, whose father had been a lawyer, linguist, and rapist, liked to say to Adelle, when she appeared looking cranky and silly in her shabby underclothes, "My father would have found it sexually stimulating to have you come to breakfast dressed like that." Today Adelle did not laugh.

So Rose, who believed that mornings were a better healer than penicillin, drank some fresh cool milk, plunged a spot-free peach almost whole into her mouth, and took a bite of leftover Persian lamb, just for flavor. It all mushed around in her mouth, and made her feel animal and alive, and happily sloven.

Adelle left for work, holding onto her studied anger, and Rose Penski stayed home, busying herself with the things of life. She checked the bird feeder and took Dollars, the dog, for a walk. Dollars was a small barrel-shaped beagle who often walked backwards on their walks just to look at Rose. The move to Fairfax had upset her, and seeing Rose made her feel safe. The dust reared up like an angry stallion, tingling the end of Rose's nose, causing her eyes to water. Dollars pulled at the leash, as snow-white rabbits climbed from underground burrows and ran in a zigzag fashion either towards or away from something, Rose couldn't tell which. A thin line of skyborne dust, a trail in the sky, traced a car approaching the house.

When they got back, Adelle was at the table looking at a heavy computer printout, her bulging briefcase by her side. "I just came back to get some things. And I forgot to thank you for making the coffee this morning." It was a silly thing to say, typical Adelle. Rose Penski had been making the coffee, each and every morning, for the past almost eight years. With temperatures soaring into the hundreds, with deaths in families, with no electricity in the house, with no Mr. Coffee filters, Rose had made the morning coffee. "No problem," Rose said, noticing that the squirrels were at the bird feeder again. "Anyway, thanks," Adelle said, and packed up and left. So it was that Rose decided to stay.

Outside, sitting by the polluted yet lovely looking pond, Rose noticed that the waters, though poison, carried the geometric patterns of the sun on small wind-waves. It seemed odd to Rose how very clear the goodbyes we say in our heads are. They are like scenes from a Spielberg movie where little is said, even less is done, and there is space galore in which to accomplish it all: the sky looms large, but soft and safe. The same old questions always arise when one plans to depart: should one walk off the dock in search of Daisy or stay and fish with Papa Hemingway? It doesn't matter, as long as the rules of emptiness are in control for a while. Goodbyes are always much better left to the various art forms. In day-to-day life, it's the getting on that counts.

Two weeks ago, Adelle's routine mammogram, a procedure which both she and Rose had been undergoing for many years, raised suspicions in her doctor's mind. She had suggested Adelle have a new one taken at a more sophisticated hospital in San Francisco. Rose and Adelle had been planning a vacation, so they rented, for three months, the little house on one of the many Fairfax hills. The San Francisco mammogram, taken the day after they arrived, had been misplaced by the hospital, giving Adelle time to read up on breast cancer with her usual fervor for the mathematical truths. Both Rose and Adelle knew she should be moving with great haste, but the lost X-ray seemed to give permission for the mountain of knowledge in the medical schools in the area to be poured over. The bottom line seemed to be that all answers were vague, that, hard as it was for Adelle to accept, little is known for certain about cancer, how to best treat it, how to cope.

However, in some silent non-spoken way, in spite of the lost mammogram, everyone knew there was a lump that shouldn't be there, even though its photo was floating somewhere beyond today. So Rose Penski made fancy dinners as Adelle read out loud from the medical journals, smiled at Adelle's existence, and watched the pond slowly become more and more overtaken with the slowly moving pollution which was killing it.

The mornings, after Adelle had left and Rose was alone, were cool, a soft fog hanging below the tree line, drifting up from the ground. By noon, however, the fog had been eaten away by the sun and the full heavy weight of summer pressed down. In the oppressive heat Rose made Adelle gourmet dinners, enjoying how her body sweated in the non-air-conditioned house, the sweat making her feel like Julia Child, dripping with pleasure and spicy smells.

After a dinner of spinach roll with mushrooms, Javanese pork done on the grill, a pear crumble pie, Adelle, sipping on a glass of sangria which splashed happily in a chilled long-stemmed glass, agreed that she should demand another mammogram at once, not wasting time waiting for the lost one to be found. They decided, later on in the bed, the paddle fan a cool wind downward and making the sheets ripple like sails on the bay, that Adelle would go alone.

"You stay behind, Rose. You know how long waits upset you. You stay behind and make me a blueberry pie. Yes, a blueberry pie with a browned flaky crust, and a glass of cognac to sip on afterwards."

The night gathered itself around the small house in what was a protective hug. The dog snored now and then, sometimes scratching an imaginary flea in her sleep. Adelle curled into a small package of fatigue, while Rose watched the whiteness of the moonlight spill over the lake, over the treetops, down to the road.

* * * * *

13

Adelle went alone to the breast cancer clinic to have the mammogram done. Later, at home, over the cognac and blueberry pie, the sun still an angry circle of red, she told Rose what it had been like.

The clinic in the foothills of Berkeley was a small home converted into an office. It was actually a small cabin sitting peacefully in a grove of eucalyptus trees, a tear-sized trickle of a creek requiring a bridge to the walkway.

Adelle gave her name and sat down, taking a few things out of her briefcase to fill the wait. No sooner was she settled than her name was called. Asked to leave her briefcase in the secretary's area, she went to put on the gown, open in the back, which had been handed to her. The inner waiting room was filled with women of all ages each in a similar gown, all silent, all leafing through the endless supply of magazines in racks on the walls. She spent most of the day there.

"We were put in a room together. Very therapeutic — we were forced to talk to one another. Didn't work though. I refused to interact. We sat, hospital gowns clinging to our breasts, holding onto our chests for dear life, reading *Redbook* and *People* magazines. I only read the articles on homes — decorating them and such."

Rose felt for Adelle. She could see her sitting, looking stern, pretending she was there to research the latest buying trends in young home buyers. When Adelle wasn't allowed to hold onto her briefcase, was forced to take part in life on life's terms, she turned hard, like an orange rind left in the sun.

"I hope the mammogram comes out well, Adelle. I truly do."

"Hope is for cowards. What I want is success."
She drained her cognac as if it were water, not even
coughing at its bite, not even taking a gulp of air.

"Then I stand corrected. I wish you success."

The sun fell with a jarring suddenness and there
was a film of night following it, catching the earth as
if in a mighty net. In that funny piece of time, that
time when the sky was neither moon nor sun, when
it seemed up for grabs, and bats replaced the birds as
riders of the air, Rose Penski always felt a chill in
her back, a lowdown chill which seemed to come from
within. The pond, drained of sunlight, drained of
moonlight, looked like some huge discarded tire tossed
out on the road by a passing truck.

Rose held out her hand to Adelle, and Adelle,
misreading the intent, smiled. "Yes, I'd love another
drink." She handed her glass to Rose and
absent-mindedly rubbed her breast as the moon broke
open upon the pond.

* * * * *

Adelle had the most disconcerting manner of
waking up that Rose had ever seen. She would bolt
upright in bed as though slapped by a giant hand,
glance around at the alarm with total fright, stare at
nothing for a moment, and then lie back down
without a word. Rose Penski herself was a quiet riser,
one who seemed to melt out of sleep.

Lovemaking, if it were to occur, was usually a
morning activity. Their approaches to it were as
different as their approaches to most things. Adelle,
after five years of a rather lackluster marriage, had
begun reading sex manuals. In all those years, her

15

husband, his freckled body shaking with pleasures she never knew, assumed that women just 'responded differently.' He would, after the act, hold her dearly, whispering phrases to Venus, overjoyed at the closeness of their union. She never told him that what she mostly did when the urge was upon him was to count the number of hairs on his chest as it moved above her. When the divorce came, when he walked out the door and into the arms of a registered nurse who giggled and called him 'Pooh Bear,' Adelle searched, not near and far, but merely near, and chose a married salesman, a man with wispy white hair and a wife of twenty years, to usher her into the joys of sex.

Like some teen-aged beauty queen after the star football player, she centered her attentions on the befuddled man, ripping him from his serene life of daily dullness. She pulled him, chapter by chapter, through all the wisdom which the sexual sages of the ages had amassed. Under her guidance, he and she assumed each position carefully, methodically, and with great determination. Though they happily followed the poses set by the blissful nude models, the act was the same as it had been with her husband — not much of anything. Jim would explode with passion, amazed at his role in life, as Adelle would wonder if she had, perhaps, missed a sentence somewhere, had placed her hips a bit off center on the pillow upon which she rested.

They made love on mountain tops and in the depths of shady coves. They made love with a vigor seldom known, indoors, outdoors, with and without props. Each union was part success, part failure. Jim was living a life beyond his wildest dreams. Adelle

16

was chasing a phantom. Once she and Jim flew to New York on business and did it in their seats, under a small airlines blanket. That one Adelle had made up, one of her own imagination. She was proud of it though it was, from her standpoint, a failure. It helped Jim, though, get over his fear of flying.

At some point it occurred to Adelle that things might work better if she and Jim were married. There was still a touch of the Puritan in her. So, while checking out some property in New Mexico, at a Taco Bell near Taos, Adelle threw down the gauntlet. "Marry me, Jim." She took a large bite of her soft-shelled taco and looked at him coldly. It sounded like a command.

He seemed befuddled, at a loss. He looked back, and took a bit of his crisp taco. They both chewed for a while, gathering their thoughts. "I'm married, Adelle. Have been for years."

"Get a divorce."

"I don't want to."

They were both silent for a moment.

"Okay then. Let's go to a pornographic movie."

They went, but Adelle found that she felt differently about Jim. When he began to finger her breasts during the film, she brushed his hand aside, and ate her popcorn with a vengeance.

A few days later she met Rose Penski.

* * * * *

Rose had learned at a rather young age that sexual fulfillment was hard to achieve in the arms of a man. She knew this not just from personal experience but also from countless interviews with

17

contemporaries. Once, after her mother had a few too many gin and tonics, Rose Penski even thought she heard her confess to a lack of success in the arms of Rose's father. Rose never followed up on the conversation, preferring to leave some truths muddy.

Rose had chased the dream, though not with the dedication of Adelle and had had only one success after endless trysts. Stopped once at a long traffic light at the corner of Lexington and Fifty Second Street in a fancy car with a man whose name and face she has long forgotten, she was fondled in a bored manner, her privates explored beneath her size five pure silk John Weitz slacks. That was in her early Bohemian years, when she was trying to experience everything in life so that she could become something great — perhaps an actress, perhaps a composer. It had seemed to her at the time that one had to amass a great deal of varying experiences if one were choosing greatness as a career. At that time in life, there was no *Ms* magazine to correctly direct attention to those experiences from which a young woman might benefit.

Rose Penski did not particularly enjoy her experience at the corner of Lexington and Fifty Second Street. She felt the location was a bit tacky, that it did not hold up well as the locale of one's entrance into adulthood. Also, she heard later that the man went to jail a few weeks afterwards for something as mundane as a crime in a bookkeeping department, fraud of a monetary nature. It did not sit well with a seeker of greatness.

After a large number of other attempts at a useful use of the male, Rose Penski gave up her pursuit of that side of the human species, for it was clear that success did not lie in that direction. All of them: the art director, the floorwalker at Saks, the dancer in Camelot, even the bartender at O'Henry's, left much to be desired. As a matter of fact, no one ever even matched the incarcerated bookkeeper.

Rose found her satisfaction, finally, in a bed which flung itself out of a wall in a small San Francisco apartment where she had gone with a friend to feed a cat. While she and Bonnie coaxed the cat into taking a taste of genuine home-cooked chicken livers, the wall bed, as if having a life of its own, would fall from the wall each time a streetcar labored by.

After putting the bed back into the wall for the third time, a "K" car rounded the bend sending it hurtling back to the floor. Bonnie laughed. "Oh *merde*. It must be a sign. Forget the damned cat and come here." She flung her clothes onto the chair by the window, and, naked, oozed onto the bed. She spoke some French which Rose didn't understand, and by the time the cat had eaten the livers, Rose Penski was in love again.

* * * * *

So, if Rose and Adelle were to make love, it was generally a morning time event. There would be no violins playing; time would not stand still. They would, simply, reach a mutual agreement.

"Want to make love?"

"I don't know. You?"

"Maybe. I don't know. Guess so."

"Okay."

Then for a while, sometimes as long as an hour, they would talk about other things, lying side by side,

19

ignoring the passing of the morning. They'd talk of what to have for dinner, the rottenness of the mail system, whether the dog needed a flea bath that day. Then, eventually, a hand would stray, a breast would be stroked, a thigh would be fondled. Talk would slow, breathing would increase. When Adelle experienced her orgasm, she would always shout, "Oh God, oh God." At first, in the beginning, this bothered Rose. It seemed out of place, not a part of them. But eventually she got used to it as a comfortable side dish, like the cranberry relish to go with the turkey.

They would, afterwards, lie quietly for a while, then the day would begin. Adelle would usually say something like, "Mmmmmmmmmm, mmmmmmmmmm, mmmmm, I sure could go for some of those yummy rolls you made yesterday." And Rose Penski would generally decide something of great importance, such as she would give up Persian cooking for the rest of the week and go Chinese.

This placid dreamlike quality was not always a part of their love-making. The first time they slept together, Adelle had awakened with her arrow-like shot at life, and said, "My mother was bonkers you know. Genuinely bonkers. In and out of hospitals all her life." And although Adelle's bedroom was the epitome of sanity, with white rugs and well-framed pictures from Africa, even a hundred-watt lamp by the bedside, Rose Penski had thought it might be wise to beat a hasty retreat. Rose was then not aware that she had given Adelle her first "big O." While Rose was trying to decide whether or not to commit, Adelle did one of the most sexy things Rose had ever seen another human being do.

20

Adelle pulled a suitcase from the closet, took a few things from various drawers, a few things from coat hangers, packed them up, and said, "I'm off to Chicago for a few days, Sweetie. Call you each night after the rates change." Then she called a cab, and waited on her stoop, dressed in red skirt and maroon jacket, suitcase used as a stool.

To Rose Penski, who had spent her entire life preparing for greatness or something like it, such a casual approach to life, such an adult attitude towards the drama of travel, was overwhelming. She was smitten. Adelle was the sense which had been lacking in her life.

Adelle did call each night after the rates changed, and Rose began to realize that for herself love was not the mad fall-apartness so often portrayed in art. For her, love was order amid chaos, answers among raging questions. Love was taking, with absolutely no fear, a trip to Chicago. It truly boggled Rose's mind.

When she went, a week later, to pick Adelle up at the airport, Adelle was still wearing the same outfit, carrying her briefcase, looking like a grown-up. Her legs looked long and lovely beneath her skirt, and she was even wearing high heels.

"Hi Sweetie," she said, and a long tired sigh fell from her lips.

It was to become a watchword, a code; "Hi Sweetie," followed by a sigh. Adelle held up until she was allowed to fall. And it was that soft fall which Rose caught, for Adelle let no other see it.

* * * * *

Of course, Adelle had a bit to learn, for it is

patently clear that sex manuals do not prepare one to be a sexual animal of any sort. Position is not everything in life.

When Adelle returned, she invited Rose to attend a business getaway her company was sponsoring to help the executive staff regroup their energies, revitalize their talents. It was held at a secluded Boy Scout camp high in the mountains. Aside from a daily morning talk from the head honcho about his personal relationship with God and how it related to real estate, the staff was pretty much allowed to commune with nature or a god of their own choice.

Salesmen and women, brokers, even a few well-placed secretaries, attended classes in yoga, glass making, basket weaving with natural fibers, or eating off the land for health and happiness.

Rose and Adelle, due to the small number of persons attending, shared a lodge which was designed to hold two dozen scouts and two counselors. The shiny knotty pine of the walls lent an air of cheer, while the huge walk-in natural stone fireplace in the center looked awesome and serious. A few Smokey the Bear posters hung on the walls, and a calendar with a religious theme was tacked to the bathroom door. There were thirteen bunk beds, none with bedding, lining each side of the lodge. Adelle and Rose viewed the room with its abundance of beds and laughed together.

"Which one do you want?" Adelle asked as she put her suitcase on the floor.

"All of them," Rose Penski replied as she put the paper bag containing a toothbrush, T-shirt, and underwear change on the floor in the bathroom.

One of the ways Adelle had dealt with her

22

sexuality and its dysfunctioning during her time with Jim was to take as many classes at the YWCA as she could. This season she had begun ballet and had learned to execute a pretty good imitation of a swan on a lake of ice.

So it was that as Adelle and Rose viewed the gigantic array of beds, all empty, all available, Adelle began to dance. Rose stood, riveted to sanity, as Adelle began to leap up and down, flaying her arms about in a frantic set of motions. As her speed increased, her eyes clouded over. Spittle flew from her mouth. She was muttering the names of the steps beneath her breath, and finally, caught up in the bird imagery she was portraying, she began to cluck like a chicken.

Suddenly, in a puddle of fatigue, she stopped, looking proud but tired. She plopped down beside Rose. Out of breath and heaving heavily, she said with great pride, "That was *Swan Lake*. We learned it last week."

Rose Penski was at a loss for words.

* * * * *

When Adelle regained her breath, she reached out and took Rose's right hand in hers, holding it between hers. Her touch was very soft.

"This is very brave of me, to take you along on a business weekend. You must realize how very conservative my company is. We sell to families, those who fear God. I want, though, I want us to be a unit. I want us to share everything. I feel very scared asking this, but I'd be more scared if I didn't ask. Scared that you might leave. I am a part of many

23

things: my mother's life-long addiction to medication, my sterile work with the company, my father's empty soul. I probably have a hundred skeletons in my closet, and I might use you to keep from dealing with them. But I will love you, with a staunchness you will find amazing, and I will be willing to put all my eggs in one basket. I have spent a lifetime being lonely, being drenched in it, and I know it's been my own fault. Loneliness is the scariest thing about me. All I can give you is a promise to try to share, to try to let you in. I've tried before, and always failed."

Adelle had consumed a few beers at the luncheon picnic that day, a few plastic glasses of slightly warm white wine. Her wild dancing had brought it all to her head. In a word, she was tight.

She continued, "I am scared, very very scared, doing all this. My company might figure it out. I might lose all I have."

Rose Penski had learned long ago that most people spend little time thinking about other people. She had noticed that since she and Adelle had arrived to flaunt their sinful ways, no one, except for a polite hello, had even spoken to them.

The speech touched Rose, and she thought it might not be so bad to spend the rest of her life with Adelle. She would dance a mean *Swan Lake* and could pack a suitcase in the beat of a heart. Also it seemed she might be willing to seek truth, to chase change. Rose decided.

"Adelle. I want you to do something for me, with me. Are you willing?"

Adelle countered with a question, "What?"

Rose counter-countered, "Will you?"

Adelle softened. "Maybe."

This was to be their rate of exchange for years to come. Rose took a wooden ladder and climbed to a top bunk. "I want us to make love in every bed in this lodge. I want us to make love differently in each and every bed."

Adelle, who obviously had one more cluck in her, did a short version of *Swan Lake* and joined Rose in the bunk. Thus began their night of bunks. There was no pattern to the choice of beds. Carrying the ladder and Adelle's nylon sleeping bag, they did each one. And Adelle's readings served her well.

That night they made love in twenty-six different bunk beds at the expense of the oh so conservative company. They finally fell asleep, exhausted from both sex and ladder climbing, as, in a distant Boy Scout lodge, the president of Adelle's company was getting ready for bed, his chosen bunk far away from his wife who snored.

* * * * *

The next morning in the main cabin for breakfast, eating pancakes too thick due to an overabundance of white flour and covered with a syrup so cold that it stuck like pebbles to the cakes, Rose and Adelle spoke aloud of their Night of Passions, as they called it. And, of course, no one knew what they were talking about.

"I was," Adelle stated, making eye contact with an elderly broker trying to get the salt shaker to pour, "most taken with number four. I found it to be intellectually stimulating, and yet pagan enough to touch the origins from which we all sprang." The broker, her white hair nicely wild, smiled, for numbers made her feel safe.

"I," Rose countered, "was most taken with ten, for it seemed less constrained, more cosmic. But, still, it was safely limited as to expression."

"The point I plan to make, when the opportunity presents itself," said Adelle, looking very serious, "is that numerative advantages are not indicative of value, per se. Circumstances must be considered, however frivolous the subject."

The broker, trying to listen, trying to catch the drift of things, began to look uncomfortable. "Would you please pass the syrup?"

Rose, bubbling with happy silliness, could not contain herself.

"What —" And she could only guess at the dangers her questions might unearth, "is the absolute value of forever? Can we cull it into a marketable commodity? Can we rip it apart and grind it down to its origins? What, I would love to ask the learned and experienced women and men gathered here today, is the meaning of forever?"

The gentleman across the table smiled in a way which did not involve his eyes, and put the butter dish in the exact center of the table, saying, "Our newer homes have a lifetime guarantee." Rose and Adelle watched as he stood up. "Ah," he said, "time for a dip in the pool." The table, draped in an oilcloth version of red and white linen, hid the light punch which Adelle gave to Rose under the table. All

26

three stood up in unison, smiled at each other, and left via separate exits.

Later, Adelle and Rose hiked deep into the piney woods, with richly scented shadows jumping madly from small bright sunlit treetops. They sat on the itchy pine needles, feeling cold in body but warm in spirit. Adelle held Rose's hand, and a few small robins pecked for bugs amongst the needles. "For the first time I know what they mean when they talk about feeling close to nature, Rose. It's not feeling left out of the world." Rose Penski, who knew a few things about life, did her imitation of blackbird calling across a shallow lagoon, and the bugs began to bite.

* * * * *

The doctor had Adelle set up another appointment a few days after all admitted the mammogram was lost. There were to be four specialists involved in Adelle's cancer process: the internist, the radiologist, the surgeon, and the social worker. Adelle was to meet with them one at a time, bits and pieces of her life being dealt with in bits and pieces.

As the years passed, Rose and Adelle had between themselves a very definite pattern for parts of days. Each day, no matter what, Rose would get up first, bathe, walk the dog, make the coffee, read the paper, and, about the time all that was over with, Adelle would come down. Rose would hear Adelle begin her shower just as she, Rose, was about halfway through the paper. Then, in the overhead bedroom, she would hear her walking from the bathroom to the closet, back and forth, picking out her clothes for the day, holding them in front of her at the mirror, brushing her teeth, holding her clothes in front of the mirror again to make sure it was all put together as she wished.

Rose liked being the first one up. She liked to get clean, talk with the dog, fill the bird feeder, and walk into the morning, whatever the weather was. In Fairfax, the morning was split. The sun seemed to hide from the house, but on the walk with Dollars, it found them, often smacking Rose with a blinding dazzle. She thought of the sun as making a statement: "I am, therefore you think."

When Adelle finally came down, the day would begin for Rose. Adelle was a part of it all, like the sun, like the pond. Until Adelle arrived, it was all slightly ajar, slightly empty.

Adelle would come down to breakfast, wearing her grayed nylon slip, but with a fabulous outfit waiting upstairs, and the dog, still happy from her morning walk, would go over to say hi. The dog knew to just sit, thump her tail on the floor, and breathe with vigor. Adelle would always shout, the noise seeming too filled with energy for the quiet glow of the sun rising, "No, bad dog. Down." Adelle would then pat Dollar's head as the energetic beagle tried to be calm about the day's beginning. It was a ritual they had established. Then came the ritual with Rose. Adelle always began her talk to Rose with the single question, "Well?" It needed no answer; it merely signified that the day had begun.

Adelle would pour some cream into her coffee, take out whatever was heating in the microwave, sit down, open the paper, and read in utter silence for a while. Sometimes she'd find a bit of something, a crumb, in her mouth and she'd move it around with her tongue as she read. All this while, Rose would remain silent.

Adelle would look up as if Rose had spoken, and say, "Yes, I know. Don't play with my food." She would then chew whatever had been on her tongue, look at the ceiling, and define it. "I think it was a bit of almond." Adelle speaking was a signal that the day had begun. They would talk about some part of the paper, comment on the weather, make small statements about the plans for the day, the evening.

The newspaper might have shouted some terrible headline, or hummed that the world had slept in peace. Still, whatever went on out there, out in the world, Rose and Adelle had their ritual, had their own morning.

Things would heat up. "Did you read the article, the one about —" Rose Penski, not allowing Adelle to finish, would know the one she meant and say, "Yes."

When Adelle had finished reading (and she never read the whole paper), and Rose began to look as though there were things to be done, Adelle would stand up, gaze off at the mist-covered pond and say, as she did each morning, "I'm going to the office now." She'd put her dishes in the sink, not washing them, then she'd shake her head slightly, as though something had just occurred to her.

"Give me a kiss. I've got to get going." It would always be a silly kiss, sort of a Dagwood running out the door kiss. As Adelle drove off, Rose would begin to wash the dishes and wonder what the day would be like.

* * * * *

Some days Rose Penski was overcome by a deep bone-drenching sorrow which seemed to hang from her soul like Spanish moss from a Florida pine. Days such as those, often days when it rained, Rose wondered what, if anything, life was all about. Rain would thrust its evil tongues at the seemingly vulnerable panes of glass, and she would wonder along with Dante, "What is, else not to be overcome?"

If Adelle were to die, it would be a slow death. In the days before hospital-controlled deaths, it was possible to die with one's boots on. Now death could only be courted in the arms of green-walled institutions as a small metal bed clacked against black-speckled vinyl tiles with each stab at immortality.

Since Rose's father was a linguist, she had grown up watching her father and his books, seeing them as a single unit. She would watch him, the thin gold-rimmed glasses tight behind his ears and pinched over his nose, and wonder if his face might snap in two. By the fireplace with the San Francisco chill heavy outside, Rose's mother long since in bed, he and Rose would sit, a quiet magic filling the room.

"This," he would say, moving a page with such love that Rose for a long time believed that all the love in the world could be symbolized in the turning of a page, "this is the ancient Egyptian sound for 'eu.' " Then his long slender fingers would point to a picture of a bird walking. Rose Penski would sit, transfixed. On the coffee table, face up, was *The Egyptian Book of the Dead*, its dark green binding

30

looking like water in the Nile River. Her father always smelled like warm bourbon and Camel cigarettes, and she disliked sitting too close to him. It awed her to know that a picture of a bird walking had a sound. What power there must be in knowing such things.

Once Rose's father had smiled her a sad smile as he sat with his pens and papers scattered about him on the floor, the cold lamplight shining on his shoulder while the light from the fireplace made hot white spots on his slippers. "Look Rose. Look. This is your name in Egyptian." He drew a snake which seemed to lick at a bird walking over some wiggling lines near a woven basket.

Since those days, Rose Penski had read *The Egyptian Book of the Dead,* though in English, not in the original as her father had. It made no mention of hospital walls, of the red light by the bed to be pushed if help was needed, of the TV set hanging from the wall which played football games and quiz shows while life stood still, stone still, in the hollow of the heart. Rose had given Adelle a copy of the book, but Adelle was still reading all the available materials on breast cancer, and had placed it in a pile of things which included things such as a letter from Greenpeace and a formal note from some political organization which began, "Dear Friend of Ronald Reagan."

* * * * *

In the midst of the rain, when the early evening danced a dance in the ugly drenching downpour, Adelle came home from work and decided to take the canoe out on the pond. Adelle knew nothing about canoeing. She knew, really, nothing about water. She could not swim very well, and getting her face wet turned her into a frightened child.

The canoe was long, very long, and a deep red, with the legend Straight Arrow written on the bow in white cursive letters. It was a fiberglass canoe, not heavy, but heavy enough that the walk to the pond made it begin to feel heavy. Adelle zipped herself into her yellow life jacket, brushing away the rain from her face with full hand motions, like human windshield wipers. She had cut a finger on some blackberry bushes while getting the canoe out of the shed, and as she wiped her face, a watered-down trickle of blood washed pink slid past her lips. The blonde ringlets of her permed hair held cupfuls of water, making it look thick and copper-colored.

Adelle put her face in gear, looked quite angry, and pushed the canoe into the water. There was no dock, just the end of the land and a lot of tall reeds. As the canoe entered the water, bumping up and down against a submerged tree truck, the grump-grump-grump of its entry was thudding. Adelle put one leg in, yelled for Rose to hold her steady, took Rose's hand for balance, and fell into the canoe with a hollow sound. The pond had no current, no flowing waters to erase its pollution, so the momentum from the fall sent it away from shore, Adelle prone, her water-stained face filled with frustration. Adelle sat up, leaning on one arm, her voice rising in panic: "Rose. Rose! A paddle. Hand me a paddle!"

Rose stood on the shore, the dog barking in excitement next to her.

"I need," cried Adelle again, as the canoe bobbed a few inches from shore, her anguish mounting, "a paddle."

Rose Penski, though the rain was much less dramatic in her own thin brown hair, had to laugh one of those laughs which only the titans of the Earth ever dare to laugh.

"Are you, my dear Adelle, are you —" And here she laughed so hard that the dog stopped barking and began to lick her ankles, "up Shit's Creek without a paddle?"

"Oh fuck," said Adelle, in her yearly use of a swear word. "I just might be." And then she began to laugh along with Rose.

It took awhile to rescue Adelle from the clutches of the mighty Gitche Gumee, but rescued she was. They had hot tea with dinner, cupping their hands over the steaming cups to feel the warmth.

"Would it have helped if you had died of suffocation in some germ-infested pond?" Rose asked. "Would you feel good knowing you had cheated a hospital bed, clean white chart by its side? Will it be the bugs of outrageous fortune which carry you off just to show the men in white what powers you possess?"

Adelle played with a small piece of raisin from the warm rice pudding, and stifled a sneeze. She seemed lost in thought. Adelle put the piece of raisin in her mouth, swallowing it without seeming to know what it was.

"Rose. All my life I've thought that as long as I worked hard, did what was expected, saved money, it would be all right. Somehow that would be it. Now that I might be dying, I wonder about all the books

33

I've not yet read, what it would be like to be a male and have all those instant meaningful relationships which men are so good at, at least in print. Instant fatherhood, after deserting his children at their birth, picking up the pieces of their lives in their teens, never missing a beat. 'Proud of you kid, you're lovely and brilliant.' But, if it doesn't look too cool, a quick retreat, and Mom's to blame. Rose, what is the answer, or, what is the question?"

Rose was in her element, for, as a philosopher she had a question for each and every situation. She was also in a state of great relief that Adelle had not succumbed to the briny depths. To her credit, Rose did *not* ask, "What do *you* think it's all about?" Instead she said, "Remember the time your father came to visit and was helping you clean up a rental during some staff strike? Remember how he said, his bald head mooning the night, Oven-Off dripping from his gloved hands, 'Shore hope this gal keeps her pussy cleaner than she kept her oven'?"

Adelle did recall, with a wan smile, a worn smile.

"Now Adelle, and this is important. Did you laugh?"

"You were there. You know I did."

"And Adelle," (here Rose paused for dramatic effect although the thunder spilling down from heaven beat her all to heck), "Here's the rub. Are you not a dyed-in-the-wool, card-carrying member of the Women's Liberation Movement? Have you not been so for many a year?"

Adelle, who could get into anything given enough clues, said loudly, "Hallelujah sister, yes I am!"

"And, as such, do you see anything even remotely

humorous about a male pig speaking of the filth he perceives to be a part of the female vagina?"

"Even if he is a blood relative?"

"Even if."

"Nope sister, you are right. That man is *bad*."

At this point Rose beat her foot up and down on the carpet for emphasis, raising her voice: "And is this man, this low-life beyond compare, is this penis-dragging, cock-hauling, heavily-laden-with-lust male, a direct descendant of, and stick it to the center of, your family?"

"Yes!" And Adelle scaled her answer to the highest domes in operatic palaces around the world. "Yes, this penis-dragging, cock-hauling, heavily-laden-with-lust male was, and God help me, still is, my very own father. He is the daddykins who wrapped my little cotton sheet around me just before he went to call my mother a cunt and rub warmed mayonnaise on her breasts. He is the font of my knowledge in all my relationships. Daddy is my dearest, my dearest of all." Here Adelle's voice lowered. "At least he saw enough in life to tough it out. He lived, lived somewhere far away from us, while our white-framed house with the smell of freshly baked apple pies wafted from the window sill, died, the diapers still on the line, the dinner still warm in the oven."

Rose cried, for life is more a feeling than a noun. "Do you need a hug?"

"Yes. I need hugs and hugs until all the arms in all the homes in all the universe decide they have as much love to give as Cliff Huxtable, and even then I need more. I need you to hold me to sleep, and back

35

to life, to blunt my needling questions with non-thought. I want to have my Mommie and Daddy back, and my little warm blanket and the funny happy smell of warm pee, the sweetly sour smell of milk on the pillow under my head. I want to live, because I haven't, and the rules I worshiped so are like Nazi tattooing on my heart."

Bedtime was a soft affair, though Rose had one of the few headaches she ever had in her life. And both their pussies, thank you Daddykins, were clean and soft, and smelled as sweet as the sheets on baby's bed.

* * * * *

Rose and her mother did not get along well, but in truth no one seemed to get along well with Rose's mother. As Rose was growing up, she had thought that her mother might be making sense, and therefore had tried to fit into the tight angry world which her mother created and called Rose's childhood. Rose used to sing and whistle happy tunes no matter what, pretending that the seven dwarfs were near and woodland creatures were on her shoulder. She made it a point to have everything done long before her mother asked. At age twelve she made her first baked Alaska, because it seemed like something her mother might enjoy. She didn't.

Rose's mother used to do things such as put the butter in the oven and the potatoes to be baked in the refrigerator. Rose always waited until her mother came back from the store and put the groceries away, and then Rose would check the kitchen. The coffee would be in the bread box, the bread in the potato bin. Once, when Rose was out, her mother couldn't find the can opener (which was in the bathroom), and took every dish in the kitchen and smashed it against the wall. Rose grew up believing that few things in life made sense.

Every morning, as the fog spilled its cold murky anger over the San Francisco dawn, Rose would get up, make coffee for her parents, set out their clothes for the day, then sit by the wall heater waiting for pandemonium. Life would issue forth from various rooms, all of it yelling and ranting, except for her father who always sat quietly and drank his morning cup of bourbon as life went wild around him.

Years later, after her father died, Rose mentioned her father's early daily dose. Her mother, typically, yelled. "Why the hell didn't you tell me? No wonder he had so many problems if he started off the day that way."

Which, even though Rose had by now spent many years under the bridges of life, made her wonder if her mother had ever, really ever, been all there. Since Rose had watched her father stumble off to work each day, it was hard to imagine her mother saw another picture, another reality.

Rose Penski's mother read murder magazines all the time, though she was too embarrassed to buy them for herself. She would send either Rose or Rose's father down to the drugstore at the West Portal tunnel the first of each month, and Rose or Rose's father would come back with a stack of gory accounts of rape and ravaging. Often her mother would shout with an odd joy, "Look at this Rose. Look. Caryl Chessman said the same thing about his mother that you say about me. Isn't that something?"

37

Rose was in her early teens when she read an article in *Seventeen* called "Your Father Wants To Love You." It was then that Rose decided to share her feelings with her father, which is what the article said to do. As she sat beside him in the going-home traffic, she stopped counting the utility poles and took a gulp. "Father. I feel scared. And sad. And even worse, nothing seems to make sense to me."

Her father, his eyes never moving from the traffic in the lane, reached over and pushed the button on the glove compartment, saying with emotion, "My baby." Rose watched his slender fingers, the same fingers which handled books with such love, curl lovingly around a pint of Jack Daniels. He took a swallow and handed the bottle to Rose. "Keep it out of sight. The cops around here are on the take and we'll pay a piece if they see it. Try it, but don't tell your mother."

Cops and mom. Rose took a sip, found it hot and bitter, and went back to counting the utility poles. The beauty of the Bay Area sunset was lost as the heated up cars spewed exhaust into the redness of the dusk.

Cops and mom. Rose thought of her mother and father as in love, but felt that some vital link in their communication had fallen, unseen, into a distant sea. It was as if, within the relationship, things had gone electrically wrong, leaving bolts of passion to writhe around without proper outlets.

When her father died, Rose had thought of that day and the hot flat bottle of Jack Daniels hidden in the glove compartment, of how that was the only time she had tried to talk to him on her terms. Her mother had scattered his ashes along a beach in Maui because, she said, "That old bastard would sit and talk that Hawaiian gibberish to those old bastards who loved the language and had so few people to talk to." As a matter of fact, Rose Penski had watched her father sit, drunk as a skunk, barely hanging onto a beachfront park bench, speaking the ancient language as though he'd been raised on poi. So Rose's mother had taken the ashes, walked up to her knees in the Hawaiian surf, and spread Rose's father on a gentle wave, and shed not a tear as she did. "Now you can jabber to your heart's content, you bastard."

Later, when Rose Penski's mother was telling her about it, she said, a glass of wine in one hand, the death certificate in the other, "You know, Rose, I loved to torture that man." And she laughed a laugh so wrenchingly real that Rose knew a bit more about the depth of her mother's soul than she cared to.

Years later, some mother-daughter filled time when the starlight was dancing on elm leaves and the sweet smell of the sea air was blowing in the back door, Rose, laughing and high on life, said, "Mother, remember the time you said you loved to torture father?" Rose laughed as she said it, expecting a hearty guffaw in response. But her mother merely looked at a beetle moving on the cement, and said with such certainty that the sky seemed to tremble, "It never happened. That never happened."

* * * * *

Adelle and Rose had a relationship with firm boundaries. Adelle went to work each day, stayed too long, and came home loaded with papers. From the time she got home until the time she left the next morning, unless she was eating or sleeping, she moved the papers around a lot, made phone calls, and wrote a lot of numbers on legal-size pads of yellow paper. Aside from those papers, she felt no callings upon her person. She would dip into Rose's mothering stew of life as she needed to, and never wore slips which were sexy.

Rose, daily, would shop for and cook all manner of nurturing meals. Pies cooled in kitchen windows, breads baked in ceramic loaf pans, pots were filled with sweetly smelling combinations of meat, spice and vegetable. There was always plenty of cool fresh milk in the refrigerator, ready to go with the homemade chocolate cookies piled high in the cookie jar. The salads were served in sparkling glass bowls, overflowing with avocados, tomatoes, segments of Mandarin oranges, alabaster-white hearts of palm, and three or four types of lettuce.

Rose cooked with both eye and taste. She carried James Beard, Julia Child, and Bert Greene on her apron sleeve. Oddly shaped green items found in Oriental markets on the seamy side of life kept her happy for days on end. An unheard of spice would send her into a cookbook frenzy. The strain of a tune from a foreign land would result in a table piled high with tidbits she could barely pronounce.

Once, when a flu bug had bitten Rose, she had sent Adelle out to the store for three ripe tomatoes. Rose had planned an easy meal, one good enough for a sick stomach: a light salad with a yogurt dressing, browned eggplant rounds spilling over with melted mozzarella cheese, and iced tea with ginger.

Adelle was gone for two hours. She came home

with tear-stained cheeks and no tomatoes. Rose said, rather testily, "Well, where *are* the tomatoes?"

Adelle sat down with a heaviness which made the bed shake. She wailed, "I couldn't find them. Where do they put them?"

Rose had spent a lifetime or two dealing with such inabilities. "Probably," she said, fighting off an urge to wipe the tears from Adelle's eyes, "probably they took all the really ripe ones, the ones which *looked* good, and hid them behind the Colombian coffee. Markets are like that. I always, as a matter of policy, look for the fresh fruit in the two-for-the-price-of-one day-old bread section."

Adelle sat, heartbroken, her sorrows masking the fact that she might be angry that Rose was sick.

"Should I," and here her lower lip quivered and her eyes became heavy with the sad dew of funeral-goers, "should I have just *asked*?"

"I think," said Rose, "had I been in that market with its glaring neon lights, I too would have stood, confused, crying copious tears. I would never, and I swear this with all the sweat collected upon my fervered brow, I would never have looked in the fresh vegetable section, the one right by the entrance."

"Oh Rose," moaned Adelle, slipping her size ten feet out of her size nine and a half heels, "I wish you had been there."

They did without the tomatoes, and the meal was fine. Rose felt better. Adelle ate more than her usual amount, saying, "I know I'm not the sick one, but this certainly makes my tummy feel better."

* * * * *

Rose and Adelle lay in bed, the early morning blues falling softly on the pond. The birds sang, clear and clean, sounding like the smallest and thinnest of bells.

When Adelle wanted to talk, she became a physical entity. She allowed her body to fall, either into bed or elsewhere, across or on top of someone, mostly Rose Penski. She became heavy, pregnant with her unspoken thoughts. This morning she lay atop Rose, much as the mist lay atop the pond.

Rose sat up, fearing suffocation.

"You must be very scared," she said. Adelle had an early afternoon appointment with the surgeon. He would be going over the possible surgeries available should the mammogram indicate a need.

"I guess so. I guess I am. I suppose so. Maybe. I might be."

"Can I help?"

"No, not really."

That was enough sharing for Adelle. She got up and began to empty things. She emptied small containers into large containers, and those into even larger ones. She emptied waste cans and pill bottles. She threw out piles of newspapers. She washed the bird feeder, and took all the dead leaves and branches off the small patch of lawn in front of the house.

If Adelle could speak her soul, cry out her anguish at the horrible and disgusting fear that she might die, she might have left things unemptied, might have looked for solace in arms, not acts. She might have gone down by Cold Shadow Creek and watched the water spiders walk, like Christ, upon the water. She might have let the shadows cuddle her with a calm coldness.

As it was, she ate, bathed, dressed, and stood composed and staunch on the stairs, her briefcase with its broken handle clutched under her arm. "I'm off."

"Drive carefully. Please drive carefully."

"I may be home early or late. That is all I know at this point. I'm not sure. Depends."

"Drive slowly, and watch what other people do. Use caution."

Adelle tripped as she came down the steps, recovering her balance with a look of fright. "If you are saying I might hurt myself, you are wrong, just dead wrong."

Adelle's car took off in a cloud of dust, Rose's words about caution as unheeded as a Just Say No poster. Rose Penski went to sit by the pond. It would be a long day.

Early afternoon, as the sun sat belly-full in a heated sky, Adelle called, which was a rare event if she was at work.

"Everything okay?"

"Just fine, Rose, for a lousy day. Can you believe the guy who's supposed to fix my computer hasn't showed yet? The mail, if you can believe this, hasn't come, and not only that, the secretary is out sick." Adelle went on and on, and Rose let her talk, waiting for Adelle to mention the surgeon, but she said, "Well, gotta go. Here's the computer guy."

"Adelle, wait. Wait! What happened at the surgeon's? What did he say?"

"That pisser cancelled." Adelle hung up.

Rose decided to walk to Cold Shadow Creek with Dollars, and took along a can of beer to drink on the way. It was very unusual for Adelle to swear.

* * * * *

Adelle did not know how to get mad. At times
when she was consumed by rage, her face would get
red and pinched, her bottom would draw up with an
inner tightness, and she would say sweet things such
as, "Isn't it a lovely day? Isn't it just too lovely?"
When Adelle talked that way, Rose knew the shit was
about to hit the fan.

Adelle was quite angry that she might have
cancer. For the week it took the surgeon to
reschedule her, she looked red and pinched, and
everything was "lovely."

When Rose got mad, she was mean. She kicked
the dog, smashed works of art, called down the
angers of Thor with a vengeance. It was clear she
was mad. She always heard herself when she was,
always saw herself. It was part her mother's ceaseless
rage, part her father when he had been drinking.

Although Adelle was foreign to her own anger, she
and Rose had lived together so long that she allowed
herself to get angry in front of Rose. It was not the
kind of anger most would notice. Adelle would stare
at Rose for a while, usually playing with a part of
her own face or arm, and then say something much
too loudly, such as "Did you water the plants today?"

Rose knew, when Adelle asked such things, that
the answer was not important. The plants were not
important. Rose could make any reply, and Adelle
would leap out of her chair, almost knocking it
backwards in her haste, and scream as though an
outrage of great proportions had just been committed.
"NEVER MIND. I'll do it, just like I do everything
else around here." Then she would water every plant

unlucky enough to be in sight, dousing them with water as though to wash away a lifetime of sins.

Sometimes Rose thought it was funny when Adelle got mad like that. But Adelle had been mad for a week now, and Rose was getting tired. Also, the plants were very wet.

That night, as the paper-thin piece of moon hung in the sky like a bitten off fingernail, Adelle said, so softly that Rose had trouble making out all the words:

"I heard, Rose. I heard about the mammogram. There is quite definitely something there. It's actually larger than it seemed to be on the one which got lost. It's been sent to the surgeon."

The bugs singing in the heat of the night made a sound much like a slowly twirling boat propeller. Rose and Adelle held hands.

* * * * *

Reading anthropology always comforted Rose. Darwin, it seemed to her, had one of the sweetest heartbeats the world had ever heard. She never saw the world in quite the same way after she took *The Voyage of the Beagle. Origin of the Species* helped her to feel the incredible glory of all things great and small, to know the clockwork of the clouds. What she enjoyed the most about anthropology, the part of it which truly touched her soul with religious peace, was that it spoke with such quiet certainty about individuals as groups. Phrases such as "the women of the tribe," or "the stick-propping characteristics of the central plains Indians" helped Rose to feel, as it were, that some eye is on the sparrow.

45

Rose was one with Ishi when he took a small step from behind a languid brook and truly walked several centuries. It was not that she harkened back to the theory of the noble savage. It was, simply, that she longed with all her being to drink water from a leaf out of necessity, not choice.

Anthropology, like philosophy, took whole cultures, whole sweeps of time, without seeming to lose a single cell of an individual. Medicine, on the other hand, seemed to reduce individuals to nothingness. Medical books, instead of showing a person proudly standing atop a majestic ravine, showed withered bodies, faces blocked out with black rectangles. Something as simple as chicken pox was made to look like the wrath of an insane god, a small child's chest shown in grotesquely unreal colors inspiring only disgust. The focus was on disease, not people, not any person. There were no names of glory, no people of the plains. There was no past, not even a body beyond the illness.

Rose Penski went with Adelle that Sunday morning to the No-Name Bar in Sausalito, an aging landmark with outdoor seating, and a brunch menu in line with the sophisticates who frequented it. The short ride from Fairfax was pleasant in the mid-summer warmth. The sun seemed trapped in the early morning dewiness, and even the ants crawling over the outdoor tables seemed to be still married to the night, marching to a different drummer than they would later when things warmed up.

Rose, although it was early and most people were asking for bagels or omelets, knew what she wanted:

a corned beef on Jewish rye, with Dijon mustard, mayo, and coleslaw *on* the sandwich, kosher dills, two of them, on the side. To drink, Rose ordered a lite beer in a mug filled with crushed ice.

Adelle, looking at the menu for a time longer than it takes most people to fill out their income tax forms, ordered a toasted garlic bagel with lox and cream cheese, plus a cup of coffee, black, and a glass of orange juice.

They watched the sailboats in the bay, and the slightly fog-kissed air felt cool and peaceful against their faces. Rose was about to take a bite of her sandwich which was thick with filling and smelled inviting, when Adelle, ignoring her bagel, suddenly covered her mouth lightly with her palm, looked oddly away from Rose, and whispered, as if to a potted palm somewhere in the distance, "Don't look now, but I think my surgeon is at the next table."

Rose moved her head slowly, wiping the coleslaw from her lips so as not to flaw the occasion. At the other table sat several tall and tanned co-eds, each kissed with the early morning energy left over from a night of love. Each seemed to be in a deep discussion about Hegel or Marx, and under the seats were straw baskets filled with French bread loaves still fresh from the morning ovens, flowers of muted lavender, and bunches of grapes hanging over the edges.

"Where?" asked Rose in a whisper.

"There."

Rose Penski then noticed a pleasant looking older man eating a danish and leafing through the movie section of the *San Francisco Chronicle*. A woman many years his junior, bearing two cups of steaming hot coffee, sat beside him, and took the business section.

Adelle looked away. "But of course I'm wrong. May I please have a bite of your sandwich?"

Rose Penski had learned many years ago that no matter where they went to eat, no matter what food was brought forth, Adelle would be drawn, in some hopeless, hapless frenzy, to whatever was on Rose's plate.

"Adelle, you haven't even tasted yours yet."

"I don't want it just now. Why don't I take it home and eat it later? I just want a taste of yours. What kind of mustard did you get? I wish I had thought of a sandwich. Is it roast beef?"

"Corned beef."

"Oh, my favorite. I didn't *know* they had corned beef sandwiches here."

Rose Penski knew this was a battle of wills, or, at least, of taste buds. Adelle would develop a deeper and deeper need to devour Rose's breakfast. Adelle took a bite of her bagel, lox and cream cheese, and pulled a long horrid-looking fish bone out of her mouth. "Look at this. Can you believe it? I can't eat this. It needs to be looked over with care. I'll take it home. Just give me half your sandwich."

Rose Penski knew that Adelle had not brought along a fish bone for such a purpose. It must have indeed been in the lox, so the battle was lost at once, even though with little prompting Rose always gave Adelle her food. Rose pushed the sandwich towards Adelle.

Adelle was not looking. She spoke, again in a

whisper, again with her palm in front of her lips. Her eyes were turned towards an invisible James Bond.

"There," she said, gesturing with her eyebrows, "see the man with the woman in pink shorts? I think he might be my surgeon."

Rose thought the man looked more like an English professor. He had hair three months in need of a trim, and one hand with long nails indicating he played a stringed instrument.

"Adelle, you met this man once, and the meeting was short. You handed him your medical report, he thanked you, you left. What are you doing?"

Adelle took a huge bite of Rose's sandwich. "Silly me. Wrong again."

Adelle had her bagel carefully wrapped in napkins and in her purse. The corned beef sandwich, with trimmings, was squarely in front of her. Rose Penski, never one to give up, said in a voice not offensive, but perhaps too loud, "The hills are alive with the sight of surgeons."

This caused Adelle to swoop the corned beef, pickles and all, into her already food-drenched purse, stand up, yawn, and say to no one except perhaps the ants, "I think we should be going." And with that she left, leaving Rose at the table with no food, the ants, and a real curiosity as to how many surgeons were actually in the restaurant that day.

* * * * *

Adelle liked to make lists. She also liked to keep files. She had files for everything. Seldom-heard-from friends would call at the hours normal folks are watching TV or taking evening walks, and ask Adelle if she had this or that income tax form, this or that rental agreement, this or that blank will. Adelle always did. People used to comment how wonderful it must be to live with such a well-organized woman. They would say with a smile, "I bet you have the most thought-out, well-planned lives on Earth."

Rose had a quest, a quest spawned by Walt Disney movies and MGM productions. She longed for a picnic — the perfect picnic. Adelle would gather information about a site, a task which might take as long as a year to complete. She would make labels: Florida, Gulf of Mexico, State Parks. She would put them into stacks, then into piles, then into the drawers of her file cabinets.

Now that they were in Marin County, a place ripe with picnic possibilities, Adelle had put all the California information on the extra chair in the dining room. After dinner, as the sun sank behind the banks of the pond, she would thumb through the materials, spreading them out on the table as Rose did up the dishes.

"Here's a nice place. It sounds lovely. I'd really like to go. Listen to this: 'The sand dunes go on for as far as the eye can see.' It even says that dogs are allowed if on a leash. Want to go? You could pack one of your spiffy picnics and we could leave early Saturday morning, spend the day, then eat at a shoreside fish buffet place on the way home."

Rose contributed to the dream. She bought coolers of various sizes and colors, containers (some costing as much as fifty dollars) for keeping hot things hot and cold things cold. She bought colored plastic plates and flatware. She bought mats to sit on, pillows to lean on, floats to float on, and grills to cook on. She made, in her head, dry runs of the perfect picnic. They would dine on chicken wings skinned and turned inside out, bone left in for ease of handling, dipped in tempura batter (dash of baking powder for lightness), and served sizzling hot with a sauce of sake, freshly grated ginger, turbinado sugar, and Old Swan soy sauce. The accompaniments would be mind-boggling: deviled eggs made square with a Japanese gadget bought at Cost Plus in San Francisco, kiwi fruit slices and mango shafts dipped in white chocolate, pasta salad made of shells stuffed with crab meat and blue cheese, with bits of fresh basil and freshly grated coconut, and, to wash it all down, fresh pressed lime juice with papaya pulp bathing in finely crushed ice with just a splash of creme de menthe.

In the nearly eight years that Rose and Adelle had been living together, they had never been on a picnic. They had planned them, prepared for them, even dreamed about them. But they had never been on a single one. Of course, they stopped at rest areas dotting the major interstates, pausing to walk the dog and take a bite of whatever Rose had in her lacquered baskets. They had even spent weeks *near* wondrous picnic areas, their papers and picnic gear in tow. But they had never been on a planned, executed, and enjoyed bona fide picnic.

Now that Adelle might have cancer, Rose Penski looked at it all with different eyes. Picnics bespoke of a happy carefree life; the sands of Waikiki, the mouth of the mighty Mississippi, the shores of the Suwannee River. It seemed that some future anthropologist, had she spoken of the discovery of a picnic dig, might

51

write, "The colorful picnic paraphernalia complete with directions for use, well-worn map fragments, sat in the corner of the empty truck, the sun-bleached bones of the picnicking family reaching out in endless yearning."

Rose, kicking a lavender and lime-colored cooler, said, "I think I'll just get rid of this shit." But instead she wiped a bit of dust off its top.

Adelle came in just at that moment. "Ah, my little picnic friend. Just what are you planning for our next outing?"

Rose said, maybe even meaning it, "I think I'll go Hawaiian."

Adelle looked pleased. "Sounds yummy, as always."

* * * * *

Rose wanted to help Adelle. And she knew that the only way to help anyone is with love. Old but true: love does cure all.

Every morning in Fairfax, as the mist moved up from the pond in small wisps, and the already warming sky mingled with the dawn peeping over the hill, the birds which Rose fed daily would flock around the feeder. There were squirrels hanging upside down slurping up seed the way vacuums slurp up dust, skittish little chipmunks, fat-faced and friendly, eating the seeds which fell to the ground. Even hummingbirds came, dancing like swirls of sunlight, looking for sweetness.

One day a huge yellow dog came by, looked at Rose through the sliding glass door, and sat down under the feeder. He wagged his tail and looked at

Rose as though it was all quite clear to him what she needed to do. His tail mashed the pansies which had been planted with such care. When his eyes touched Rose's for an instant only, he rose, his massive golden body happy with life, and pushed his nose against the glass. After that, Rose began to take him on the early morning walks she and Dollars took.

He would run ahead of her and Dollars, but come back every few moments for a pat from Rose or a sniff from Dollars. Rose named him Gulliver. Both she and Dollars were glad to have him for a friend. They would all return from their walk long before Adelle arose.

Rose Penski would sit, sipping coffee (actually she gulped everything in life), reading the latest madness warlike males were inflicting on other warlike males, some of them even her countrymen.

Later, with Gulliver outside, his tail leading some of the most majestic symphony music in the world, Adelle would come down, her eyes amazed that the world still existed. Each morning, without fail, no matter which creatures danced or sat right outside the windows, Adelle would say, "Well, well, well. It looks as if we're all here. You certainly have a following, don't you, Rose? Yes, you certainly do."

Then she would get some vanilla-flavored coffee, drench it with cream, pick up a section of the paper, and stare at it as if it were shrinking.

"I really might need glasses. May I borrow yours for a moment?" She would say this without looking at Rose, holding out her hand. Rose Penski would pass her the glasses.

Although Rose wanted to help Adelle now, with her diagnosis such a terrifying thing, she knew it is hard to help others. There is a danger in it. Anthropologists know this. It is called interfering with the life of the village. Rose knew that something as simple as suggesting Adelle get her eyes checked would only force Adelle to say, "What a good idea. I guess I should get my eyes checked." Of course, Adelle would never do it. She always acted as though problems would disappear if one ignored them.

Adelle wasn't acting that way about her possible cancer. She was moving as fast as the system would allow. This time it would not pay off to ignore the problem, and Adelle knew it. Rose Penski was proud of Adelle for changing the whole pattern of her being, for moving right into the heart of the problem, even though the fear was overwhelming.

She looked up from the *Chronicle* and made eye contact with Rose, a rare event for the morning. She shook her head, which made the borrowed glasses slip slightly down her nose. "Can you believe this? I mean, *can* you believe this? I am reading the obituaries. The daily obituaries! Seems as though the Big C is the most common reaper." She took the glasses off, and gazed out over the polluted pond. "I'm too young to be reading the obituaries." Her voice sounded thin and whispery. She took a huge bite of her apple strudel and handed the glasses back to Rose.

"I love you, Adelle. Things will work out. I have a feeling that things will work out."

"Have you," said Adelle, getting up and tossing the paper dangerously close to Dollar's face, "have you watered the God damned plants?"

* * * * *

54

Rose Penski felt about anthropology the way some people feel about want ads. She saw opportunities, ways to live, ways to think, ways to feel. Adelle made about sixty thousand dollars a year, but she never saw a side street, never saw a chance for a different way of life. She went to work, had for eons, sweated, slaved, and occasionally wished she were doing something else. But her mind never went beyond that. She never wondered if her heart could have scaled mountains, if her soul could have swum with dolphins. Adelle never dared to think that something might be wrong in her well-ordered life. She thought only when paid to, or so she claimed. Therefore, her soul was left to wonder at its pain.

Rose Penski, however, cried at the drop of a hat for lost opportunities. She had seen love, life, even meaning, swept down the gutters of the globe, and still birds sang.

Once Rose read of how Aztecs killed members of their society. Some were killed for their beauty, their ripeness, their appeal. Their hearts were ripped, blood dripping from their rib cages, to calm the madness of the sun setting, to keep the gods of life throbbing, lest the next day never start. Some were flung, dressed in finery, into murky waters, slowly sucked down to hidden caverns swarming with dark-blinded fish.

But Rose thought the worst of all was the killing of the drunken Aztec. In the Aztec society, the priests' power over the people rested in knowledge, so it was that knowledge was guarded, hoarded. Only the priests knew how to make wine. It had to be that way. So when a hapless Aztec somehow stumbled on the tastiness of fermented fruits, became a little tipsy, felt a slight loosening of spirit, the priests struck him or her down. The drunken Aztec was slain for simply knowing a bit too much. The guise of concealment worked then, and it works now. One cannot steal secrets from the gods.

Adelle and Rose took the dog for a walk. A few rabbits were on the landscape, standing still, white against the dark earth. Dollars barked at them, pulling at her leash, which was in Adelle's hand.

"Would she kill one if she caught it?"

"Maybe. She's a beagle. She might want to play, but instinct would take over. They've been bred to catch rabbits."

"Do you think humans are molded by instincts?"

"More than is supposed, I would posit."

"Rose. He's going to chop off a part of me. Should I be scared?"

The clouds broke open, and the rain began to pelt. They arrived home, wet and dripping. The kitchen table was covered with books and journal articles about breast cancer. They hugged each other.

Rose sat down to read, and Adelle stopped at the refrigerator for a snack.

"May I eat the remnants of this wild rice and mushroom souffle?"

"Have at it."

As most cooks do, Rose loved to watch an eater eat. There was something so warm and loving, so animal and nice about the whole process.

Suddenly Rose screamed, causing Adelle to jump back from the plate in fear. "Adelle," Rose cried, "you're eating the rice with the pooper scooper!"

It was the only time in her life that Rose Penski heard anyone actually talk comic strip language.

Adelle threw down the large old spoon and said, "AAAARRRGGGG!"

* * * * *

Adelle could and did reduce all things in life to questions. She would never say, "The day is lovely." Instead she would say "Isn't it a lovely day?" It was, Rose thought, Adelle's way of feeling safe. And, of course, it forced people to respond to her, to answer. "Yes. It is a lovely day. Quite lovely."

Some people ask questions to gain knowledge, some to confuse and befuddle the listener, some to stall for time. Adelle had no rationale to her questions. Like a shark in a pool of blood, once started she became frenzied and unable to stop.

Going to the movies with her was sheer hell, a true lesson in terror. She would munch her popcorn, her head held forward inches beyond her shoulders in an effort to truly become part of it all. In a voice too loud she would spurt out questions between her popcorn chomping.

"Was that the same red car the killer was in?"

"Was the man we saw before the lawyer or the janitor? Was he wearing a wig?"

"Did the safe open because the wire was lit?"

Eventually Adelle would become befuddled by her own endless questions, and wail, "I don't understand," in a voice loud enough to cause row upon row of annoyed patrons to whistle "Shhhhhh" in unison.

Adelle could take pages of realty facts and reduce them to a single coherent statement. She could write a financial package which was a joy to behold. She

57

could do that and much much more. But she could not, when in the company of another human being, refrain from asking questions.

Rose Penski, therefore, became an expert at answers. She could answer questions almost as fast as Adelle could throw them out. If a movie was total confusion to her too, she could even make up answers which fit the plot.

However, the questions which Rose Penski liked to ask seemed to bore Adelle, driving her to work on obscure pieces of month-old junk mail, to compile one of her lists, to clean a counter top.

Rose Penski wondered, often aloud, why death and horror seemed so close at hand, and what could be done. She wondered why that most valuable of commodities, love, slipped so slyly through so many hearts, both individual and corporate. Rose had another question, one which she carried daily in her heart. Had her parents ever loved each other? Some idiot voice in her always answered no, but that was not enough of an answer.

But mostly, of late, Rose wondered how Adelle could face death if she had to. Would she try her old trick of asking questions, or finally form an answer of her own? As it was, Adelle seemed to be dying a death per day, sometimes more. Occasionally she and Rose would be somewhere, on the beach, at the pond, then, from somewhere deep inside, Adelle would scream a muted scream, one which the wind cupped up and moved away. Rose would say, softly, "You just screamed, Adelle. What's wrong?" Adelle would answer, annoyed by the question and somewhat puzzled too, "Did I scream? Did I really scream? How bizarre. I didn't hear myself."

Rose sometimes felt herself drowning in Adelle's questions. She wanted to be there for her, make the muddied waters clear, wanted to give what hangs so heavenly-heavy at our fingertips. Adelle often looked at Rose saying nothing, the sun falling, perhaps with sorrow, into the reflections on the pond. Dollars would lick imaginary creatures off her paws, then a big hand would smash the sky, making room for the moon. Moved by the beauty of life, Rose Penski would plan, would think how to make things better. Adelle would shake her head slightly, asking, "Isn't the reflection on the pond lovely? Will we have artichoke hearts in our salad tonight? Was there any mail today?"

And Rose would spew out answers, forgetting her own thoughts, though of course the night was lovely.

* * * * *

Adelle's father, Evan, was a friendly looking man although his nose was a bit sharp and his mouth seemed a bit small. He always wore the whitest of T-shirts, and his almost totally bald head was made electric by the flashing of his deep brown eyes. He wore false teeth which he usually forgot to clean so that, unlike his T-shirt, they were yellowed. He didn't really fit the picture of a lady killer, but women were the major occupation of his life.

When Adelle's mother had relapsed for the third time, when her addiction robbed her of much of her brain, Evan left. Adelle, though left with only her demented mother for nurturance, was always quick to condone his desertion. "I would have left too. He did the only sensible thing." Adelle talked about Evan as if a jury were listening, as if she had to defend him against silent charges. She never saw that she was the one judging. She never questioned why he hadn't taken her when he left.

The truth, as Rose Penski saw it, was that Adelle would have walked over hot coals bare-footed just to have Evan cook up some shrimp scampi for her, boil her a West Coast crab. He was, though, everything, literally everything, she hated in a male. His favorite line was that he had spent his life trying to "get into as many pairs of panties as he could." He would even say, when he'd downed too many beers, that there were a lot of little kids out in the world who bore a striking resemblance to him. Adelle always laughed when Evan talked like that.

He did not take kindly to the relationship between Rose Penski and Adelle. He did not believe in relationships which did not involve a penis, although he loved to withhold sex from his wife for any of a number of small reasons. As a matter of fact, he often said with pride that she hadn't had any for twenty years. "Don't want to spoil 'em, make 'em too happy."

Rose once said, "You *really* do love Evan, don't you?"

Adelle pulled at her bra, looked confused, and asked, "Who do you mean? Evan?" It was hard for Adelle to take things in. Once Rose and Adelle had gone to an art show with all manner of art upon the wall. Rose lost Adelle for a while, and finally found her staring at a wall with nothing on it, a simple brick wall. She was a mere inch from it, and seemed lost in thought.

Rose went to her side. "Adelle. What are you doing?"

Adelle smiled. "Just enjoying the art."

"Adelle," Rose Penski had said with a touch of pain, "you're looking at the wall."

Adelle had seemed pleased with the information. "Oh, that's what it is."

With a little help from Rose, they moved on. Together.

Whenever Rose Penski tried to talk about the bond Adelle felt towards Evan, Adelle would become disgruntled. "Bond? Do you mean sexual?" Rose wouldn't answer. "Just because," Adelle would snort, "just because I once saw Evan naked doesn't mean a thing."

Rose always asked the same question. "What did he look like?" Adelle always answered the same way. "Well, his penis sagged a little, sort of like a bag of beans. And his pubic hair was white." Rose would then always ask, "What color are his eyes?" Adelle would look as if she had been asked how many hours there were in a day, and would blurt, "Blue of course. River water blue."

* * * * *

Rose did not trust people who really loved food. Like all who enjoy cooking, she enjoyed those who praised her food, who dug right in. She always had liked to make people feel good in their guts. But there she was, as she saw it, a bit of strangeness about people who were wedded mainly to food.

When Rose was little, her father used to sit at the

head of the large dining room table. All the food would flow from there. First would come the salad bowl. Her father, never batting an eye, would pick out each piece of avocado, each radish half, take a small piece of lettuce, and send the rest on to his family: lettuce leaves and celery slices. He would carve the roast beef with loving care, pile it high upon the serving plate, take the choicest bits, and again pass to his family those pieces which were too fatty, too well done.

When Rose had read *The Diary of Anne Frank,* she knew that had her family ever been forced to hide in an attic, her father would have eaten all the precious bread, sucked dry all the eggs.

Adelle hid food. She would take gifts which were given in love and tuck them away. Rose Penski learned that if she ever craved a piece of white chocolate, a yogurt-covered raisin, all she had to do was look in Adelle's underwear drawer.

"Adelle," she used to say before she learned about people and food, "I will be glad to buy you whatever you want. Name it, and it will drip from the cabinets, bulge out at the seams from the refrigerator."

Adelle's bottom would get smaller. She would huff and puff. "I," she would say with a red face and a look of feigned fatigue, "I just put the remnant of that candy bar behind my desk calculator because I thought the ants might get it if I left it sitting in the kitchen." Once Rose got Adelle over six pounds of white chocolate, hoping it would be enough. Adelle took it all to her office, and it was never seen again.

Rose gave Dollars treats: small bits of rawhide shaped like tennis shoes, bits of crackers shaped like bones. The dog would look pleased, wag her tail, and take the gifts on the run. The treats would always show up under a pillow somewhere or behind a sofa.

Rose hid things too. She hid bits and pieces of herself, and like Adelle and Dollars, she had a hard time remembering she had done so. At times she would get up in the middle of the night and wander along the path the moon made on the carpet. She would follow a shadow in her mind, hoping to find the part of her she missed that day, the part she had needed and couldn't find. One part was so small, so vulnerable, so young. One part was Tarzan, always saving the wounded, swinging free. One part was James Beard, busy in the kitchen. One part was Dracula, looking for a throat to call home. When Rose Penski would walk the moonlit paths on her rugs, she would wail to herself, "Oh. Oh. Oh."

The moonlight was always a gentle source of warmth for Rose, though it warmed nothing but the soul. It was the spotlight of life. She would catch the moonlight in her palms, and in so doing hold a million of her dreams. She would lick her hand, lick the moonlight from it, trying to catch it, but it would be gone, having fallen silently back to the carpet, out of her reach, as Adelle slept in its shine upstairs.

Rose Penski had always loved deeply and well, if not wisely. Her father had been tall and lean, and had done everything as if it had meaning. She used to sit by the fire in the cold San Francisco nights, watching silently as her father took his glasses out of their case. He had treated them so carefully, not the way he treated people. He had hung the eyeglass rims behind his ears with such slow tenderness before he opened a book, before the fire turned to smolder. Rose would sit at his knee, waiting, knowing he would begin to read. When he did, the colors of the fire made his face fierce yet tender. Rose learned on those flame-colored nights, that books were magic.

It was still nice to know, Rose Penski would think, as she gathered the paper from the mailbox as the sun was living only in the uppermost leaves, it was nice to know that her father took the best food for himself, that Adelle always had candy hidden in her underwear drawer, that Dollars was forever putting expensive pet treats under a pillow.

Predictability was heartwarming. The bottom line, though, was that Rose Penski never knew, not even for an instant, what she would do the very next moment, or why she had done what she had just done. There was some pattern to her, but no one had ever loved her enough to see it. That thought made the moon feel cold, but, then, the sun was moonwalking down the tall skinny pines.

* * * * *

"Adelle. I can't go on. Everything I have is gone. Stormy weather."

Adelle glanced up from the paper. "What, Sweetie?"

"Adelle. Even as you sit there, you might be expiring. Although it happens to all of us sooner or later, it might be happening to you with great speed. I can't stay cool and calm. I want to hold your hand. I want to hold your hand."

"I'm aware of the fact that I might die, Rose. I just choose not to deal with it at this time."

"When, when, Adelle, my darling, my dearest, when will you deal with it? Your not dealing with it is driving me bonkers. I need to have your brain work as well with your life as it does in your business. I need to have you move and wheel and deal. I need to have you face it. We can't wait much longer. If you have it, the Big C, it is eating away at you, and each day is taking a month, a year, maybe forever. Please please please. Stop reading. There is no perfect treatment. Any one will do. Keep your brain if you must, but give your breast over to the society for the preservation of life. Give it to the imperfect male who dominates. I want you. Let's stop this war of wills."

"Soon Sweetie. I need to do some more reading. We have to wait for a few more lab tests to come in. Maybe after the radiologist's report. Maybe I might begin to make plans then."

"Plans? I'm not talking about plans. I'm talking about feelings. About taking messages to the stars, about raging at rabbits who stand still, about moonlight that moves. *Feelings.*"

Adelle fondled her chin. "I might fly to see Evan tomorrow. It would be nice, though, to have a tasty dinner here tonight."

Rose Penski, apron in mind, thought at once to cook some Cornish game hens stuffed with wild rice. "Why," she asked, "are you going to see Evan?"

"Did I say that?" Adelle seemed to fall into the landscape without seeing a thing. "Well, I guess I am. Are you going to get into one of your moods about it?"

Rose, in her mind, leaped out the window and paddled a canoe to Manhattan. She and a lover sailed the mighty Hudson River, not knowing how polluted it was, then landed smack dab in New York City.

Just as they were taking their sleeping bags and tap-dancing shoes off the barge, Adelle broke in.

"Rose?" Adelle sounded mad. "Are you going to do one of your things?"

Rose began to sing, for when the weak get going, the staying sing. She sang, her heart pouring out love, life, and perhaps (she did have a touch of honesty) some anger. She sang Porgy and Bess numbers until Adelle interrupted, getting up from the kitchen table. "Rose, one of these days I'll have you locked up. I'd like to eat early enough to allow me time to pack." She sucked a small bit of coconut caught between her teeth, and went upstairs. Rose began to prepare the Cornish game hens. But known only to her, Dollars, and the wild birds at the feeder, she kept singing, though softly, the rest of the songs from Porgy and Bess.

* * * * *

Adelle did, of course, fly away to see Evan. She did it two days before she was to have her exploratory operation, her biopsy. Rose awoke to see Adelle dressed in her black and white raw silk suit, her black Capezzio shoes which were sharper than any storm trooper had ever donned. Her hair was ablaze with the light of morning. She clutched her black leather handmade-in-Italy purse, which had a small white silk scarf falling with reckless abandon from one corner.

"Going somewhere?" asked Rose who was usually the first one up.

Adelle wiped the side of her nose lightly, so as not to mess her makeup, pleased beyond belief that not only had she gotten up before Rose, but Rose hadn't even heard her dressing. "Oh. Didn't I mention? I thought I might fly up to see Evan today."

Rose always thought that Adelle looked quite stunning when she put on her professional face, although she was just as fond of the face which stared at her over coffee each morning.

Rose didn't wipe the sleep from her eyes, but she did brush a gnat away from her arm. "I thought you said that when you went to see Evan, if you went, you'd like me to come."

"Did I say that?"

It was an old game they played, and it served them both well. Rose, being something of a philosopher, could, she thought, always see many facets in a given situation, and therefore might, and did, make differing judgments on different subjects throughout the day. Doubtless she had said she didn't want to go see Evan. And doubtless she had said that she did. She doubtless had said both things, many times. That left Adelle free to pick a statement to her liking, apply it in a situation, and say it, almost with a small kid's "ha ha, told you so," and then do as she had planned to do all along.

Rose Penski, knowing defeat all too well and all too often, wished Adelle a safe trip, and tried to go back to sleep, which was impossible. Adelle, placing her suitcase on the edge of the bed, sat next to it and touched Rose through the blanket. "Rose," she said, and her eyes looked lovely, "Rose. There is something we have to discuss."

Rose opened one eye and looked at Adelle again, noting how coiffed she looked, how adult and able and together. Adelle sat under all her maturity, and put on a face which would worry Goliath himself.

"Rose —" And her voice sounded somber. "I've put the kitchen rug outside to dry. It's been quite damp lately, and I'm not saying this in a critical manner, but I thought it might be best to let it dry out. I've hung it over the bike in the driveway, the bike with the flat tire. Please check it during the day and put it back when it is totally dry. You might want to move it from the bike later and hang it in the direct sunlight, only, though, if it remains wet throughout the morning."

Rose decided to fling the rug into the pond the moment Adelle left. She could blame its disappearance on the squirrels or some raggedy passer-by. "Don't worry, Adelle. I'll take care of it."

"I know you will, Sweetie. Well —" And as Adelle stood up, Rose was again aware of how color co-ordinated she was, black on black, all of it playing well against her rough blonde hair. "I'm off."

They kissed a small kiss which sort of fell to the floor due to lack of luster, and Adelle left. As her black heels sank into the mud patch near her car, Rose could hear her "Shit" with astounding clarity.

The dog came to the bed, licked at Rose's face for a moment, then barked a short sharp bark for her morning walk which was indeed late. It was only seven o'clock, Rose had nothing to do but take care of the rug, and she was already behind schedule. She picked up her shorts and shirt from the floor, slipped them on, and walked downstairs, saying hi to the six-foot-tall banana tree on the step landing.

As she and Dollars went outside, she touched the rug. It was not all that wet. A plane passed overhead, which she knew wasn't Adelle's. It was almost two hours to the airport, and Adelle had barely left. But Rose Penski also knew that no matter what time Adelle left, she would arrive without a moment to spare, fall into a panic thinking she had left her ticket at home, find it in the inside pocket of her purse, rush towards the gate, almost trip on something, decide she was hungry, think to stop for a bite, decide to wait and eat on the plane, get to the gate just as the last call for boarding blared over the intercom, then walk slowly towards the boarding gate, looking for all the world like a full-fledged card-carrying adult.

Rose would miss her.

* * * * *

Once, when Rose's father was still alive, she had asked if she could come watch him try a case. She liked to imagine him Perry Mason-like, destroying evil, freeing goodness. She hoped that if she watched him in action, he would stop smelling like stale urine and cigarette smoke, that he would cease to pick at angry scabs deep in his scalp, that he would not make rambling speeches about his personal hatreds. She hoped he would become suave, competent, admirable in her eyes.

The request seemed to terrify him, drive him deeply into his seat. "No," he said. "It wouldn't serve a purpose. No." Rose felt as if she had asked him the worst question in the world, which frightened her. She later asked her mother if she had ever seen her father in court.

Her mother had looked annoyed. "Don't be dumb.

Of course not. Who'd want to go see some drunken fool make an ass of himself in front of a group of people?" She moved some papers on the glass table in the living room. The table always looked greasy because, since it was furniture, she always used furniture polish on it. "Besides," she said wisely, "you must know it would embarrass him."

So it was that Mr. Penski, who spent vast amounts of his time in the public arena, was never observed in action by his family. Once Rose's mother said she'd heard a rumor that Mr. Penski would appear before the bench, slightly drunk, and speak in foreign languages geared towards the last names of the judges. Rose wondered how they managed to live as they did if her father was such a drunken fool.

Rose had once seen Adelle conduct a realty workshop entitled "Getting Them Set Up To Buy." The audience was small, made up mostly of older balding men. She was introduced by a young man in a green jacket as "A colleague of great intellectual worth, a woman who can put a fire in your sales program."

A few of the men went to sleep almost at once, but the others took notes and appeared interested. Adelle put her overheads in upside down, tripped over the cord connecting the overhead projector, and spilled the glass of water on the lectern. She read a few of her graphs incorrectly, and her embarrassed laughter touched Rose. The lecture ended when Adelle tripped over the cord again, this time plunging the room into total darkness.

Later, pleased, Adelle asked, "Well, how did I do?" It was at that point that Rose Penski knew why her father didn't want her to watch him in court. "It was great, Adelle."

The oddness of life often made Rose ponder. Once her father, on a fog-draped San Francisco Thanksgiving, the turkey nearly done, had sat his family in the living room and, resting his elbow awkwardly on the mantlepiece, had said, "I wish the assembled masses to know I am impotent." The assembled masses were Rose, her mother, and an aunt who happened to be visiting from out of town. In later years, Rose wondered what Miss Manners might have suggested as a correct reply.

Adelle's father was not impotent. Adelle called Rose from his home in Bakersfield. "We ate dinner out. I can talk now. He's gone to bed. He brought along his latest love. She was my age and wore a T-shirt which said, 'Love An Old Man, Especially His Wallet'. Evan bought her the most expensive dinner on the menu. He gave the waiter a fifty dollar tip, and called me his sweet little gal."

"Come home, Adelle."

"I'll be home late tomorrow. Evan says he wants to cook me breakfast before I leave. He says I'm his little girl. I better stay. It's important to him. Thing is, I'm not sure if breakfast will be with his sweetie or not."

Rose often wondered about the small — although it got large press — growth at the end of a man's groin. Men seemed to feel that the sun set, the moon rose, and tides swelled, all to the swing of the thing. Yet it was so vulnerable that it was protected from damage in ancient courts and in modern courts of law. Since the end of matriarchy, the penis was power — aided of course by guns, bombs, and propaganda.

Sometimes Rose and Adelle would be sitting, talking in the sun, and Adelle would look between Rose's legs, smile, and say, "Ah." It was, even after all the years, always a pleasure, a very blood-throbbing pleasure, to look at each other down there, and see it all again, as if for the first time.

Rose and Adelle got along very well without a penis in the family. When Adelle tried to turn Evan into a penis in residence, Rose often thought of her father's broken one. She wished she had said, back then, "That's okay. A broken penis is not a big deal."

However, Adelle was coming home, and it always took a while to de-program her from Evan.

* * * * *

Adelle returned looking pale, as she usually did when she visited Evan. She was still wearing her lovely outfit, only she and Rose knowing that she had worn it several days in a row.

She tossed her bag on the bed. "Hello, Sweetie."

Rose knew from years of such behavior that Adelle would not offer a single word of what the trip had been like, that each bit of information would have to be pulled with long arduous questioning.

"How was Evan?"

"Fine."

"What did you two do together?"

Adelle folded a slip carefully, though it was to be put into the dirty wash hamper, not a drawer.

"Not much."

"Was he glad to see you?"

Sitting on the bed a good foot from Rose, Adelle began to dig through her purse. "I think I left my vitamin C pills there."

Rose Penski was growing weary. "Adelle? Was he happy to see you, were you happy to see him? How did you spend your time? Tell me about it."

Adelle began to dress rather absentmindedly. She walked into the bathroom and began to brush her teeth. As small bubbles of foam oozed from the corners of her mouth, Adelle answered.

"Well, he was busy most of the time, so I sat around and read some realty materials I had with me. He came back with a female friend and we went out for dinner. Some of his male friends joined us, and everyone drank a lot of beer."

Adelle wiped her mouth on the bottom of her nightgown, and crawled into bed next to Rose. "It's nice to be home."

"Did you and Evan get to talk about your possible cancer?"

Adelle wrapped herself around Rose and tightly closed her eyes. "I guess so. He said that there have been a lot of advances, that I shouldn't worry. He said he caught over fifty fish the week before I came."

"Did he say that he loved you?"

"I think he forgot this time. He said he was working on a TV somewhere, making some repairs. I think he was wishing he was with his chickie."

Although the wind was blowing over the pond and the air smelled fresh, the night was hot and sticky. It was a hotness unfamiliar to Rose. She became wet with sweat and had to move away from Adelle.

"I'm going to get some iced coffee with a dab of coffee ice cream. Maybe even a touch of cream and a sprinkle of freshly ground nutmeg. Want some?"

Adelle sat up at once. "Oh, that sounds good."

Although they had to arise early the next morning for the biopsy, coffee never kept either of them awake. They drank the ice-creamed coffee in silence, leaning against each other in bed. Rose Penski kept a small dab of ice cream on the bottom so that Adelle could ask for it when hers was gone. Adelle's spoon soon scraped the bottom of the cup. She looked at Rose the way a puppy looks at someone eating a hamburger. Rose looked at the ceiling and sighed. "I don't know whether to finish this last little bit of ice cream or not."

Adelle said, "I'll eat it," and grabbed the cup almost before Rose could say okay. The darkness finally blotted out the small glaze of sun which still clung to the dusty edge of day.

Adelle touched Rose. "Rose. I'm scared. Would you hold me please?"

Later, when they were both almost asleep, Rose heard a shot from a rifle fired across the pond. She knew that had to be illegal. The shot of death sounded out of place in the quiet of the night. Rose Penski wondered if the man, and she knew it was a man, had killed for sport or because he disliked a particular creature.

* * * * *

Rose and Adelle both awakened early, long before they needed to. They read the paper in silence, trying to pull the morning into slow motion. Tony Perkins confessed that an obsession with his stepmother had limited his sex life until he sought therapy. Frank Sinatra and Ronald Reagan both had small growths in their colons. Peggy Lee, recovering from major heart surgery, was shocked and saddened to learn that Benny Goodman had died. A local resident who had taken part in the liberation of a Nazi concentration camp remembered that he was astounded when, upon freeing the skeletal remains of the barracks, each and every one of them had begun to walk away from the camp, not waiting for food or shoes which were in abundance. He had tried to ask one man, but the man didn't stop to talk, merely whispered over his shoulder, "We've been here long enough."

With almost an hour to kill they were still picking at apple fritters, nibbling on farm fresh strawberries, and stirring coffee light with cream and flavored with vanilla.

Adelle plucked the stem off a berry before popping it into her mouth. "Rose," she asked as she dipped the berry first in honey, then into powdered sugar, "do you think this AIDS thing might be the end of human life on this planet?"

Rose took a sip of coffee, and quickly sang an entire Cole Porter song in her head. "Possibly, but that might not be too bad. Might be time to give the other creatures a chance."

Just then Gulliver licked the window with his tongue, and Rose fell in love with him, his energy, his maleness, his entire self.

"Adelle, this is a scary thing. We are going to find out more information than we might want to hear. I want you to know that I love you. And, more than that, I love you so much that I will never pretend to know that I can understand what you're going through."

"Is my makeup on okay? Will we be too early?" Adelle began to ask questions.

"Let's go," said Rose, much more firmly than she intended.

* * * * *

The hospital, a Catholic one noted for its superior care, was short, pink, and almost devoid of windows. A mere two stories tall, it sprawled on several acres, but wound like a snake among trees, grasses, and the tip end of a public lake, finally resting where it began. It, so to speak, bit its own tail.

Rose and Adelle walked through the doors which opened and closed without a sound. Potted plants several feet tall lined the pink-carpeted hallway. A skylight spilled diffused morning on posters which advertised services: the addiction clinic, the baby clinic, the dialysis clinic. Two more glass doors and they were at the receptionist's desk. Pam was dressed in white wool, purple cotton, and several strands of gold. She was on the phone, too busy to talk. Adelle stood by the desk while Rose sat to read a *People* magazine. The piped-in music was soft rock, young men singing about love. Adelle stood at the counter, adjusting her glasses often. Pam stayed on the phone.

After Rose had leafed through January, February, March, April, and May, Adelle came and sat beside her. "They're running behind schedule." She looked blotchy in the false light.

Sofas, a soft pastel, were arranged so that no one

faced anyone, but everyone faced a TV set. Adelle and Rose watched a young man on Phil's program say that he was only twenty-five years old, that he used to be fat, but God had turned his life around. Members of the audience asked if he had ever used dope, if he dyed his hair.

Rose and Adelle waited for three hours. Patients came and went. One man limped on a foot wrapped in gauze. A baby was held with love by both staff and parents. An older man came and went in a wheelchair.

Then, without warning, just as Rose thought she might spend the rest of her life reading magazines and watching miracles, a woman dressed in a white and blue uniform entered the room.

"Adelle. Adelle Dune. Doctor is ready."

As Adelle went off with the woman, she handed Rose Penski her pile of cancer books. "Here. Hold these for me."

Doors slammed shut with energized efficiency, and Rose was left once again to the pile of magazines.

The soft rock music played on and on. Finally Rose went and asked Pam to change the station, lower the volume. Pam, who was so nicely dressed, both breasts bobbing up and down in place, said, "Can't be done. If it could, I would. Them docs like this station. I personally would rather have country. If I turn it off, the whole intercom system goes. That woman your sister?"

Adelle was lost behind the white doors for over an hour. Finally a voice, and it drowned out the TV sets and the music, asked in a strong clear voice, "Is there a Rose Penski out there?"

Rose Penski acknowledged her existence, walked

77

through the automatic doors, and was led to Adelle, who was sitting on a metal chair, a small paper gown hanging limply from her shoulders, a cup of coffee resting shakily in her hand. They looked at each other for a moment. The room was white and foreign, and there seemed no protocol for speaking.

Rose touched Adelle. "Are you okay?"

"The doctor is bringing you some coffee. He's getting some for himself and some for you. He even got me this. Isn't that nice? Physicians rarely do that."

They sat in the heavy whiteness. Adelle was shaking, something Rose had never seen her do. The doctor came in, coffee in each hand. He wore his name on his hospital coat. Having his name on himself made Rose think of a bottle of Coke. It seemed strange to wear a label. He sat on a stool opposite them. His eyes seemed kind, though covered by his studied professionalism. He had a yellow pad of legal-size paper, and his cup of coffee. He took a sip, and looked deeply at Adelle for a moment, then at the floor. His voice was low, quite soft, almost too soft to hear.

"The results are positive. The growth is malignant."

Rose Penski had once read that eternity was one ham and two people. That had seemed funny when she had read it. But his words, the still-life quality of the scene, hung in the room. There were tears, and hard breathing. Coffee was spilled. But there was no sound. No motion. Time melted, not like in a Dali painting, but the way day melts into evening. There were no hard lines. Just death and life, standing face to face.

Adelle reached for her papers, her notebooks, but Rose had left them in the waiting room. Rose took Adelle's hands, which were shaking so badly. Rose said to the doctor, "We have no questions now. We must leave."

"I understand." He opened the door for them, and they escaped from the whiteness of the hospital. There was no need for talk because the silence yelled.

* * * * *

As Rose and Adelle awoke the next morning, they both realized it was time for a picnic. They held each other in that nice manner which morning can allow, and watched life in the treetops. After breakfast, Adelle called work to cancel her appointments for the day. Rose began to cook and pack.

As the birds sang and the chipmunks scampered, and Gulliver made nose spots on the window, Rose made a picnic to outdo all the picnics ever seen in *Gourmet Magazine.* The fruit salad was lightly splashed with crushed mint and wine. The pita bread sandwiches were stuffed to the top with freshly sliced cheeses, meats, and tomatoes, all as thin as tissue paper. The never-before-used thermos held a rich cool blend of mango and orange juices, yogurt, and honey. There were slices of pan-fried apple pie, a dabble of Wisconsin cheddar grated on top. The chips were homemade, paper-thin rounds of Idaho baking potatoes, deep-fried, and just lightly kissed with salt.

Rose drove since Adelle still hurt from the biopsy. The radio was playing *Carmen.* The summer life of the trees was pulling down towards the soil. Life was getting ready, mid-summer, for winter. Adelle held her chest to protect against the pain of going over potholes.

"Rose Penski. You heard my phone call to the doctor last night. I have two options. A full mastectomy or a lumpectomy."

Rose swerved slightly to avoid a pothole. "Yes. I heard."

"I have another option."

"The biggie?"

"Yes. I may want to take a swim in the Atlantic to attend Wimbledon."

Rose Penski used her most favorite quote from Seneca. "Suicide is the only gift the gods gave to man."

"Rose. Forget the philosophical side. Suicide is in my blood. It is pretty certain that my mother's drug overdose was no accident."

Rose swerved to avoid another pothole. She muttered a swear word, and decided it probably was *not* a good time for philosophy.

After a few moments of silence, Rose took a chance. She glanced at Adelle for a moment. "Adelle. Do you know this is the first picnic we've ever been on? After all these years, and an attic filled with picnic paraphernalia?"

"When I awakened this morning," Adelle answered, "I thought that might be the case, although I didn't really formulate it in my mind."

"Adelle, look out there, to your immediate right. That is life. And yes, a person would be a fool, having no grey matter, to not think of cheating death, to not think of jumping just before the plane crashed, to not bite the poison pellet just before the bamboo was shoved under the nails. Hell, Adelle, I'd kill myself a million times a year if it weren't so final. There are religions scattered between here and holy walls which call for death as a way of life. But *this,* and I want to make this perfectly clear, *this is our first picnic.* So let us go then, you and I, as the California sky is spread out like some huge picnic table, and see what we can do to make this a bell-ringing, hell-singing, dingaling day!"

When they entered the State Park, paid their money and prepared to enter paradise, the toll taker, a pretty young woman with a ponytail, said, "Commodes are out. Bushes and what will have to do. Have a nice one, hear?"

Adelle looked about in terror, and muttered fearfully, "I have to pee. Now!"

* * * * *

And oh Lord, great God almighty, it was a picnic just like picnics are supposed to be. They ate the sandwiches so that the juices dribbled down their chins. They watched young manhood chase Frisbees, looking as important as Zeus in pursuit of truth. They watched babies cry, then laugh, then cry, then be taken into the shallows of the river only to suck in their breath, not knowing then whether to laugh or cry. They watched young women divide their attentions between the sun and the sons. They watched balls and balloons and smoke from grills, and they heard more rock music — blared so loud that it seemed to become a part of the landscape, a mountain — than they thought they could endure.

A small boy came over and looked closely at Adelle, then gave her a rock. He began a conversation

81

with her, saying that he had a ball and that he was on a picnic. Adelle looked startled. Humans, especially young ones, rarely spoke to her without cause. The boy's father came, carted him away with a soft, "Sorry lady," and Adelle asked Rose a puzzled sounding, "What did he want?"

"To talk I guess. To be your friend."

They continued to open cartons, to eat, and to smell and watch the mad frenzy that is life, human style, on a river in the summer. Finally Adelle could stand it no longer.

"I have to ask you, Rose. What exactly is the definition of a picnic? Does this really count?"

"This counts."

"But what is it that makes this a picnic?"

"Because we have defined it as such. Pass the pan-fried pie."

The sky grew chilly. Winds picked up debris and tossed it down the rocky paths to the water. Perfect, Rose thought, just perfect. To be rained out on one's first picnic was a dream come true. Even better than ants. People began to leave in small clusters. The sun seemed to fight to come out, and lose. It would be a few moments before the raindrops began.

Adelle was eating her pan-fried apple pie, looking like a person having fun. She spoke with her mouth full, words slightly blunted between the bites of apple and crust. "Do you know that a while ago, a short while ago, I asked Evan if, after he left my mother, he had ever tried to call me, tried to get in touch. He was out of my life for so many years. I thought maybe my mother did something to keep him away. Threaten him with something. Know what he said?"

"No."

"Well, he just looked bored as though it was a dumb question. 'No,' he said, 'I sure never tried to come around. Why the hell should I? Your mother was raising her skirts for everyone. I didn't want no guy laughing in my face. Woman spreads it, I shed her. That simple.' "

"I'd be angry, Adelle. He left you too, not just her."

"Well, I'm not. I understand his leaving. It's just that sometimes I feel sad, empty."

The sky grew darker, and more and more people were leaving. Those who stayed were fighting the wind for control of towels and blankets.

"I almost died once, Rose. It was on a dark slender road leading to a hellish swamp somewhere in the South. The tire blew, and my car swerved across the road. Nothing happened. There was no car coming the other way. But in retrospect I can see it was a close call. Someone *might* have been coming."

Rose felt a drop of rain on her naked knee. She didn't bother to remind Adelle that she had been on the trip with her, and that it had been about as close to death as Christians are to Moslems.

Another drop of rain fell, this time on Rose's nose. "I almost died once, Adelle. I was flying somewhere in Colorado in a small prop plane. There were just three of us aboard, when a blizzard came down from nowhere. We made it to a small landing field, but the landing gear had frozen. They were spraying the airport with foam, and we just kept circling. The only thing I could think of, when I was certain I was going to die, was that it had been nice to have lived. And I cried, not from scare, but from primitive gladness."

83

The rain began to fall more rapidly. It was soon pouring.

"It's best we leave now, Adelle."

Adelle looked surprised, even as the rain began to collect on her face.

"I thought you said picnics lasted all day."

"Not if it rains, Adelle, not if it pours. Picnics are like parades and ballgames. They get rained out."

"I was having so much fun, Rose. I like picnics. I don't want to leave."

Rose began to gather their things, and they made it back to the car just before a major deluge. Adelle decided she wanted to drive, and she drove with slowness and care. The single-lane road from the State Park was filled with those who had also been rained out. A car filled with young people tailed the car, honking and trying to pass in no-pass lanes. Finally, at a crossroads, they careened past, holding an empty pizza box out the window on which they had written with a marker DROP DEAD.

The rain splashed down from the summertime trees.

"What was that, Rose? What were they holding out the window?"

"Who knows?" said Rose and took a bite of apple pie.

* * * * *

Back home, they sat in front of the big picture window overlooking the pond, and read books and articles on breast cancer which Adelle had gotten from the medical library.

Adelle interrupted her reading to say, "You never mentioned. How did it turn out, the plane over the foam?"

"Safe landing. Saved at the last moment. The gears came unstuck."

"It's not the same you know, that kind of almost dying. They didn't cut on you, hack something off."

"You're right. It's not the same. I've never been cut on. Even have my wisdom teeth. But you can make choices about how to deal with this. Your future is up to you. My life was in the hands of fate, the pilot."

The rain made the day dark and grey, yet the colors eerily intense. The green of the trees seemed supernaturally vibrant and alive.

"Would you like to see where he cut, where he did the biopsy? I took the bandaid off when I bathed this morning."

It was hard for Rose to look. There was such a difference between a scraped knee and an incision made with forethought. It was longer than Rose had expected, almost two inches, and had been sewn closed with black thread.

They looked at it together, Adelle bending her head over to see herself. "I didn't really look at it before, Rose. I wanted someone, you I guess, to see it with me. Pretty bad, huh?"

Rose Penski became Clint Eastwood, and said with a tough yet loving look that it wasn't all that bad. Adelle closed her blouse and they went back to reading. The doctor had suggested Adelle take a week, read until she was comfortable with the surgical choice she made. For Adelle numbers were a way of life, and the doctor respected that. He wouldn't pressure her, would merely make clear that time was of the essence.

The rain seemed to creep down the windowpanes, as a snake might move down a tree. The water on the panes clustered together, then made slow-running, thick, heavy water-bundles that moved to the bottom of the sill without sound. The medical books were clinical, graphic, and depressing. Adelle stood up.

"Let's take the dog for a walk in the rain."

"Sure."

If Rose and Adelle had been different people, or if they had been in San Francisco, they might have held hands as they walked along. But they were respectful of the feelings of others, so they walked as closely as they could and still be discreet. At times their hands accidentally brushed. The rain was steady and cold.

* * * * *

Rose and Adelle began to talk more often, to talk about the long ago. They shared stories they had forgotten to tell each other over the years, and they were remembering, for themselves, the long mosaic which was their lives.

It was nice, warm and human, much like fur-coated animals which, in the depth of winter, lean against each other for warmth and comfort. Adelle seemed to be moving more slowly, more softly. Rose seemed to be thinking less, feeling more. It was one of those times of life, like a long car trip or a slumber party, where it is okay to share anything.

"Once," Rose Penski said, and this was her worst memory for so many years, "once when I was little, about seven, I was walking home from school in San Francisco. It was right after World War Two, and we had just moved back home after following my father around for his training. I was walking home alone, after a day of having no one in school talk to me, as usual. I was kicking a small rock, trying to keep it off the grassy front lawns and on the sidewalk. It was a game I made up, pretending that if I could keep it off the grass, everything would be all right. My father would stop drinking and my mother would stop screaming. Even the San Francisco fog would go away."

Adelle looked at Rose with the look of one who is really there, who is really listening. Rose was pleased, and the story began to feel less important than the fact that Adelle was listening to it.

"Then, about ten blocks from home, a car pulled up beside me. It was my mother and a friend, laughing loudly, tooting the horn. My mother yelled out the window, 'God, Rose, do you look like a fool. A total fool. I never have seen anything so damned funny in my life. We've been following you for blocks.' Then they drove on, without even asking me if I wanted a ride."

Adelle touched Rose's hand.

"But —" And here Rose smiled that famed Rose Penski smile. "Here is the good part. Every day after that, for the rest of the years I went to grammar school, even though I knew 'Step on a crack, break your father's back; step on a line, break your mother's spine' every day after that I stepped on every line all the way home. And you better believe I never kicked a rock again. So things never got better."

87

Adelle laughed. "Once," she said, "I called my father a poop pot. Not to his face, but in my head."

Rose Penski adjusted her glasses because they always hurt the top of her right ear late in the day, and decided to go on.

"Once I decided that it wasn't fair that I had to share my clean underwear and socks with my little sister just because I did my laundry on time, and my mother never got my sister's done. So when my mother asked me, on my sister's first day of school, if I had a pair of clean socks and underpants she could borrow, I said no, even though I had my usual week's supply hidden under my shirts. Later my mother found my clean clothes and said in a voice I can still remember, 'You lied. I can't believe that you of all people would lie. I'll never trust you again.' After that I hid my clean clothes more carefully."

Adelle kissed Rose lightly on the forehead.

"After my father came back into my life, when I was in my teens, he took me out to dinner once a month. I always ordered the least expensive thing, and never got a dessert. But one time, I felt brave, and asked for a steak, and even had a root beer float for dessert. I was so nervous I could barely eat it all."

Rose wiggled her toes around in her Berkenstocks and touched Adelle lightly, messing her hair just a bit.

"Once my mother said, 'Rose, take your father downtown and help him pick out his new suits. Whatever you do, don't let him get any of those awful tweed things he likes so much.' We went through a few racks at Brooks Brothers, and finally I let, yes I *let*, my father get a tweed, but made him also get a grey flannel and a blue serge. I was all of ten."

"Rose! Once my mother asked me to peel apples for a pie, and I got tired and threw half of them away. Perfectly good apples, and I threw them away."

Rose had to ask the big one. "Have you ever kicked a dog?"

"No. Of course not. Dogs scare me."

"Me neither. Never kicked a dog. Never punched a person in the nose. Never used a public restroom."

"Never peed in a public place?"

"Nope, never have. Never sat on a pot nor thought I ought."

"Why in the world not?"

"Someone might hear."

The crimes all seemed smaller. They laughed and hugged each other. Life was seeming sweeter. The days were long and soft with light, and the wetness of occasional summer rains seemed good.

When the sun came out and Rose was peeing, Adelle sneaked up and said, "I hear you."

The pathology reports had come in, and Rose and Adelle went to see the radiologist. Adelle had still been hoping that she had been misdiagnosed, that there was some mistake. No. It was cancer, in the lateral position. The radiologist, a small red-haired woman, stood beside Adelle in the examination room. Rose sat in a chair in the corner and Adelle was on the examining table. The radiologist looked at Adelle with care, and touched her softly on the shoulder. She was a woman caring for another woman, just as it had been long ago. No words or schmaltz, just a warmth and softness.

In spite of the confirmation, Adelle looked peaceful

when they left. She wore her white linen suit, a lime green silk blouse, shoes of beige with deep green trim, and carried a beige purse. Her blonde hair shone, and her eyes looked movie star great behind her green-tinted designer sunglasses.

"Well," she said.

"Well," Rose answered. And they drove home in silence.

Back home, Dollars, not knowing the knocks which life can give, was overjoyed to see them, bounding about with wild joy. She made them feel as if heaven itself must be weeping tears of joy that they were home.

Adelle changed her clothes. "Rose, I would like a drink. A stiff drink I believe it is called. The kind you so often drink."

Rose made a drink with several types of rum, several types of fruit juice, lots of ice, and the warmest of love.

They both sat back in easy chairs and watched the shadows fold over the pond. When the birds sang in the late of the day, they at times sounded like an animal in pain. Rose and Adelle listened to the loneliness of the pond, to the sounds of the birds, knowing that day had pulled itself away from their comfort. Rose and Adelle listened to each other without words, and to the sound of the ice clinking in Adelle's glass. For the longest time there was nothing but quiet and the sound of night erasing day.

The moon broke from behind a cloud, and Adelle began to speak, looking out into the gathering darkness. "I had thought, right up until today, that maybe I didn't have cancer. That there was some terrible mistake. I had thought, in typical denial fashion, that I was immune, safe from death."

"That's why they have all these checks, Adelle. Why they don't just use the decision of one person. Cancer is complicated. Much more so than I even knew."

A squirrel ran across the lawn. "Rose, I am scared. There's just no other way to say it. I am scared."

Adelle drained her glass and asked for another. Rose made this drink even stronger, even fancier: more rum, less juice, and a nicely slivered twist of lime crested on the rim of the glass.

The chill forced them inside, where Adelle finished her drink and they watched the evening news. Peter Jennings was talking about the big celebrations for Miss Liberty, about the waves of new immigrants who made up and were still making up the American Dream.

The local station gave a listing of fireworks displays where freedom and the good life would rend the skies with a powder invented in China so many centuries ago and used endlessly as a symbol of America's freedom. The newscaster looked serious: "And remember, each of these celebrations will begin at exactly six minutes after nine."

"Must have something to do with the sunset," Adelle said.

As she spoke, firecrackers a few homes away invaded the living room and knocked Peter Jennings, who had come back on, out of hearing range. Gulliver, outside, and Dollars, inside, went wild howling and barking. Rose and Adelle ate dinner to the pop, bang, and whir of America getting old. The dogs got tired of barking, and lay down to sleep. Adelle barely ate, which was very unusual. She was slightly drunk and slightly loose.

"Rose. I want to make love tonight. I want to make love more than I ever have. I want to make love to the sound of the night going mad. I want to make love and then go to sleep for the winter."

In bed, with the firecrackers still popping now and then, with the night breaking into startles of color, with the heavy-hearted boom of artillery from men playing at war, they made love. It was a long drawn out funny making of love. They laughed and told jokes. They requested, with giggles, that they not be so noisy. They begged each other for mercy, asked the dog to be quiet at moment of high excitation, then laughed at that. Later, much later, when they were holding their togetherness between the covers, when the popping of the firecrackers had stopped, when army-clad youngsters were off listening to rock, not cannons, Adelle sighed.

"I'm going to send my radiologist flowers tomorrow."

"Adelle, you have never sent *me* flowers in our whole life."

"I have so."

"When?"

"Remember those two dozen roses you got when you left forever? One of those times you left for good?"

"Come on. You mean the roses your father sent with the card which said, good luck elsewhere?"

"Is that what the card said? He never told me."

"Do you take credit for that?"

"Well, it was his idea, his card. I just paid for it."

"Well, that certainly would turn a woman's heart."

"There was another time. I think I brought you flowers from a convention once. Somewhere I went back east."

"Adelle. Do you mean the time you missed your plane because you couldn't find your ticket, so on the way out of the hotel, on the way to your four-hours-late flight, you took a carnation from the Welcome Realtors of the World floral display, and gave me the sad wilted thing pretending you had purchased it?"

"You knew it was a second-hand rose?"

"Of course. What florist wraps a single flower in toilet paper?"

They laughed.

"Maybe not just two dozen of one kind, but an assortment, a lovely bouquet. Maybe flowers each day of the week for the rest of the month. Forever."

"Adelle, have you found the mother you always wanted?"

Adelle nudged Rose. "She was nice, wasn't she, Rose?"

Rose thought a moment. "She was, Adelle. She was. Very nice. But if you dump me for her, there'll be no one to feed the dog while you're in the hospital."

Adelle yawned. "I love you, sweetie. Maybe I should send her candy too. You know these things, Rose. Does she like candy?"

And Adelle fell asleep dreaming, perhaps of sugarplums.

* * * * *

The morning windows were sheeted with water, but the rain had stopped. Humidity held the skies full, but the sun was dancing across the mists. Adelle awoke with her usual start. Rose had already bathed and had breakfast on the table. She came up and sat on the bed next to Adelle.

Adelle began the talking. "Rose. I'm still very frightened. I thought it might go away. I wonder how much it will hurt." She climbed out of bed and began to do some stretching exercises. "I'm not very good at pain."

"That's okay. No one is, really. They say animals might feel less pain because they don't think about it, don't increase it with thought. I'm not sure if I believe that, though."

"Do you think I should do some of those visualization things, where I think of my body as a white light or whatever?" Adelle was running in place, holding her right breast to keep it from bobbing up and down.

"Sounds like an okay idea. I thought you believed that was all crappola."

"I'll try anything that might help."

Adelle sat on the floor and began to stick her foot up her nose, grunting as she tried. Rose knew there was no point in talking when Adelle was into her routine.

At last Adelle finished. She took off her dripping nightgown and went into the bathroom. Rose followed. The yellowed light from the skylight made it clear that day had begun, and as Adelle took her shower, the sun splashed in the spray. Adelle as usual was washing with Irish Spring, and smelled good, just like the ads said. She spoke over the spray and the sun and the soap suds. "Do you think," she yelled from behind the spotted shower curtain, "that in the hospital if I asked you to shut the door after you come in, if I make certain security is tight, that we might make love right there in the hospital bed?"

"No. But I will rub your back, hold your hand, or sing a song that brings back life."

"Yes. All of the above would be nice." Adelle got out of the shower and began to brush her teeth, water still dripping from her hair.

Rose moved closer although the humidity in the room was almost unbearable. "Adelle, all our years together I've always said I'll rub your back, and I never have. Sometimes for a while — maybe a minute — but I hate to rub backs. I say I will and I don't. Do you know that?"

"Of course."

"You mean you knew, you really knew, that I am not a back rubber when you are so clearly a back rubbee?"

"Rose, you don't pull the wool over my eyes all the time."

Rose became pensive. "I don't know *why* I hate to rub backs. I can do almost anything else the world asks."

"Lazy, Rose. That's the bottom line. Lazy. A back rub has immediate feedback. One can't goof off. *You* can't engage in it because you might get caught smelling the roses."

95

"Lord, Adelle, what else do you know about me that you're keeping a secret?"

"You'll see. As our life unfolds and my new relaxed person takes root, you'll see, though it was never obvious, that I was there all along."

"You mean I wasn't that lonely?"

"Not for a second. You were always on my mind, you were always on my mind."

Downstairs in the kitchen they broke their fried cinnamon crisps into pieces and plunged them into the warm vanilla cups of coffee.

Adelle didn't eat her slice of honeydew. "My system is upset, Rose. I'm not hungry."

"Adelle my dear, your story is being played out in the universe. The stars are weeping in sorrow, and sending out light in joy. Planets, a few, have decided to take a few days off and not twirl because Adelle is ill. You don't have to get out of kilter. The world, the galaxy will do it for you. Eat, drink, and be merry, for tomorrow you may live."

Adelle ate, and left dressed in a wine-colored short-sleeved shirt, white silk slacks, and a scarf with just a touch of pink. Daring. She looked well-groomed, far from death. And her scarf was short enough to escape the Isadora Duncan retribution from the gods.

Rose took the dog for a walk. It was nice to move, to see the squirrels, smell nature. Sometimes it was nice to do safe things, like hold onto a hand much higher than yours.

Just before Adelle got back home, Rose remembered, in one of those flashes that sometimes occur when memories are too hard, something about back rubs which she had forgotten. She had been asked, day after day after day, year after year after year, after her father had left for work, to "Rub my back, Rosie. Just rub my back for a while." So Rose would rub her mother's back. The room, its smells making her sick, her mother moaning with pleasure — it all came back.

She was going to tell Adelle, but Adelle had her own insight to share. She took off her scarf, put down her purse, and looked excited.

"Rose. Not many people have a plan for living, a recipe. But then those who think they do often take the ingredients for a cake, put half the ingredients in one pan, half in the other, bake them both in separate pans, and wonder why they don't end up with a cake."

Rose decided at that moment to make a sponge cake for dinner the following night.

* * * * *

Rose had read, a while ago, that there was an island tribe of probably very wise people. It was their custom when a person turned forty to have a funeral, proclaim that person dead, and relieve thereby that person from having to take part in the rat race of life. Of course, that person, though dead, still slept and cried, still ate mangoes and fish baked in banana leaves, thought the same early morning thoughts and wept the same early evening sweat — but that person was thought of as a god. The entire function of that person was to give sage advice to those not yet forty. However, this was California, and although both Adelle and Rose were past forty, they were not spared the rat race.

97

Lately, the days seemed long. When Adelle went to work, Rose felt somehow lost. Things were moving so quickly, and small things added up to monumental changes. It was hard to keep up. Loves of the past often stop. People change. But when entire systems come to a standstill, it is frightening.

Life would be different from now on. Because some cells chose to go off the deep end, life would be different. Hugs would say different things than before. Backrubs might be longer. Even the kitchen would smell differently: cancer diets, cancer menus.

As a child Rose had once climbed to the top of a very tall mountain. She had gone alone. The grass was long and the sun was warm. She rested on rocks, brushed away bugs. It seemed like a forever walk. Then, at some time when the sun was sitting in a chair, not moving, just resting, she found a place at the top. Below as the Napa Valley, small tufts of clouds floating between her and it. The earth itself seemed to be broken into small patches of color, like a vast blanket covering an infant.

Rose had sat, alone above the valley, above the smoke of dusk that was day, for a long time. It must, she had thought, be how the gods felt when they looked at the infant called humanity. There it was, in its cradle, all green and growth. Above was the sun and the sky she danced in. They gave light, those sisters of safety. Even the moon, leaning on time, was getting ready to disappear.

When Rose began her descent, she took something with her. As one who has looked at a single painting in a museum, a painting complete, not spilling over onto any other painting, a painting which is just there forever in time, Rose had looked clearly at life.

And indeed, it was as small and brisk and clear as a work of art. The minds which dizzied it with confusions, the minds of the critics, the minds of the patrons, were the same minds which, it seemed to Rose, took life and reduced it to its highest problems.

At the bottom again, Rose heard a bird sing from atop the mountain where she had been. The song was as rich and clear as when she and the bird had shared the height.

As Rose thought her thoughts, Gulliver came to the window, his nose making wet spots, his tail wagging madly in the belief that he was communicating with Rose. Inside, Dollars rolled on her back and wagged her tail. It became clear that the two wanted to go for a stroll alone. Rose knew that if she let Dollars out, let her roam with Gulliver, she might get hurt, lost, killed. But he wanted her to come, and she wanted to go. They had a whole world to explore. When Rose opened the door, Dollars didn't even look back. She and Gulliver bounded for the wilds.

* * * * *

The teaching hospital in San Francisco was like most such hospitals. It had a wide array of patients many of whom no other hospital wanted. As Adelle went to get registered for her second opinion with a radiologist, Rose sat in the waiting room watching the poor bits of life which passed by. It amazed her to realize how much humans would put up with to cling to life.

Adelle and Rose wandered the long white hallways looking for radiation. It was in the basement. They got off the elevator at Level B and tried to follow the signs and arrows. Men and women, mostly black, dressed in light blue hospital garb, pushing huge dollies, joked together. The walls were cement as was the floor. Radiation therapy, overlooking the parking lot, had huge picture windows — a surprise at Level B.

As they waited their turn, a young cancer patient played a song on a computerized music board. With her father beside her correcting each wrong note, the young girl played "Twinkle Twinkle Little Star" over and over. Rose and Adelle said listening, waiting.

The nurse finally came in, smiling. "Are we ready?"

Rose and Adelle followed the nurse, who sat them in a small examination room and handed Adelle the paper hospital gown to put on. The gown kept falling open as Adelle sat on the edge of the paper-lined metallic table. Rose thought she looked so small and fragile, about to break or be broken.

The intern was the first to examine Adelle. He was a short young man was almost no chin and huge glasses. He was quite short, the sort of man who must have been teased unmercifully as a child, before brains were recognized as a status symbol. He was laden with compassion and Adelle answered his questions with ease. The only time it seemed hard was when he asked if there was a history of breast cancer in her family. Adelle always found it hard to talk about her family in front of strangers. "Not that I know of," was all she said.

Rose had never noticed that when Adelle was nervous a large section of her neck turned red. Dr. Ramey was standing as he spoke with Adelle, his body pressed against the table where Adelle sat. His head was only a few scant inches above hers.

"Should we worry about suicide? It's a thought which often comes with a diagnosis."

Adelle's neck flushed an even deeper crimson. "I have committed myself to the course of action up to and including surgery. No need to worry there. After that, I have thought of suicide as a viable option. It would depend, of course, on the quality of my life."

"Of course."

Ramey left, and Adelle and Rose sat in silence waiting for the next physician. He was *the* radiation specialist — quoted in all the books they had been reading. He was the one Adelle was prepared to trust to zap X number of rads into her body daily; he would choose the location, choose the dosage.

He was smooth. As he entered Rose noted that he had the most expertly pressed shirt she had ever seen. There was not a wrinkle, not even a crease, anywhere. It was almost as if he were wearing boards on his chest. Hissilk tie was of muted tones, and caressed his throat with a strange and compelling sexiness. His fingers were thick, as was his black shining hair. And he smiled, oh, did he smile. He came in smiling, washed his hands smiling, said hello smiling and sat down, smiling.

"Well," he said with a smile, "let's see what we have here. I'll ask some questions, then it will be your turn. Lie down please."

His examination seemed tender as he spoke with Ramey, who stood by watching. "Some hardening around the nipple. That's to be expected from the recent biop. That need not concern us. Now here, did you feel this? A node, big and hard as a marble. Did you feel it?"

Ramey ran his hand inside Adelle's underarm. He couldn't find it. The expert smiled.

"It's there. It might just have been activated by the biop. Not uncommon." He looked at Adelle, as if suddenly aware of her being. "How're we doing?" Adelle said nothing. "You may sit up now."

Adelle sat up, wrapping the paper gown about her. Her eyes looked large. Rose knew she was waiting for the expert to speak to her, state what he had found.

He smiled. "You are a perfect candidate for lumpectomy. We have a clearly defined small cancerous mass, no sign of spread. Your breasts are not pendulous, though they're not small. The cancer is lateral, which will reduce the scar area. The choice is up to you."

Adelle took the ball and ran with it. "If I were to get a lumpectomy —" She covered her body with a rather regal swoop of her arm. "Would there be anyone you might recommend to do the radiation therapy?"

The expert took a seat next to the table. He looked silently at Adelle, smiling widely. Adelle took the hint. "Would you have time to do it?"

The physician reached into the pocket of his pressed shirt and took out a card. "Here's my card. Think about it and let me know."

They shook hands, and he left with Ramey. Adelle got dressed, talking all the time. "Rose. Have you ever seen a doctor give a person a business card? It's almost as though he's recruiting people, selling a product."

She talked all the way to the car, asking herself

questions which she pretended were meant for Rose. And Rose wondered how Adelle was coping so well with so many choices to make, her dear Adelle who had trouble choosing between roast beef and pastrami.

* * * * *

Ron and Nancy sat on Governor's Island, the sky bursting behind them, the wind blowing their hair. Frank Sinatra and Shirley MacLaine, having given up being Democrats along with Ron, beamed and smiled and were proud to be Americans. The sky blew itself away and the happiness of freedom cascaded from the mouths of the rich, the richer, and the very richest. Rose's grandparents had come to America via Ellis Island. She sang along, always having had a spot in her heart for hoopla. Adelle went upstairs. "I'll see you when it's over." Adelle went to bed and Rose watched all of it, the entire celebration of Miss Liberty and her celebrity friends. When Rose finally went upstairs, Adelle was sitting bolt upright in bed, reading a cancer book.

Rose sat gently next to her, and took the book from her hands.

"Adelle. Tomorrow we are going on a trip. Where is that place you always wanted to go but never had time for? Wherever, we'll go there. It's less than a week till surgery, and the change of scenery can help you make up your mind about which operation to opt for, which radiation to go with. What say?"

Adelle looked happy, which surprised Rose. "Mendocino."

"Tomorrow," Rose said, "as dawn rips the sky to shreds with the star we all love the most, we are going. So be forewarned. Get your Northern California file, find some numbers, and make us a reservation. I'll be back from the grocery store five minutes after it opens tomorrow, throw a few things together, and we're off. You don't have to be in the hospital for six more days. Thank heaven the physician you have chosen had to be out of town until then. We're not going to sit around here and read any more cancer books. We will get out there on the road with America. Hellfire and damnation. It's about time we become one with the great outside. Let's get rolling."

Her patriotism and the speech exhausted Rose, and she climbed into bed next to Adelle and fell to sleep right away. Adelle took advantage of the fact to sneak a few more chapters in.

* * * * *

True to her word, Rose had things ready to go less than an hour after she got back from the store. She had bought a flank steak, a whole chicken, and some pork tenderloin to cook once they arrived. In case there was no fresh fruit available up the coast, she bought apples, nectarines, cherries and a watermelon. Before Adelle was bathed and dressed, she had made taboolie salad, marinated vegetable salad, and cucumber/Bermuda onion salad with yogurt. She packed homemade trail mix, and thermosed up some iced tea with mint, and some apple cider with a stick of fresh cinnamon. Of course there was plain water for the dog. Car snacks included carrot sticks, celery stuffed with chive cream cheese, tortilla chips with hot sauce, and finger-sized sandwiches on cheese bread: corned beef, chicken salad, baby swiss with dill pickle slices, and bacon, lettuce, and avocado with tomato.

As the sun hit the pond, they hit the road. They took Highway One most of the way, and it was lovely. They stopped along the way now and then, watching waves smash against rocky cliffs, watching smooth bits of sea spread out with gentle peace. They ate their lunch at Manchester State Park. They found a place to set down their picnic blanket, in use now for the second time in history, and Adelle, fighting the light wind which kept pushing the road map against her face, said, "Yes. Here it is. We're headed in the right direction." She folded the map and began to eat. "I can hardly wait, Rose. I want to dine on whitefish, and watch the sun fall up and down, like some deranged yo-yo. I want to watch clouds play leapfrog with each other."

"Adelle, you don't talk that way."

"Ah," said Adelle with a smile, and talking with her mouth full in typical Adelle fashion, "but the new me might. That is how Rose Penski talks, and I want to talk that way. I want to see nature as a part of life, not something on post cards. I want to find perfection in living, not in working. I want to move like a flag in the breeze, the message not counting, only the beauty. I want to wave."

Rose watched Adelle and was touched. As always when Adelle reached out to life, Rose wanted to hug her, touch her, protect her. "Let's go, Adelle. Let's get this show on the road."

Adelle stood, raising her arms and facing a patch of redwoods. "I want to, dear mother fucking damn, I want to be alive before I'm not."

And off they went, the sky both behind them and before them looking blue and soft. They found the little bed-and-breakfast place for which they had reservations. The owner, Pat, was dressed in a tennis/beach ensemble of white crumpled cotton. Her skin was dark against it. She had the leisure dark tan which only blonde athletic-looking women get. Her eyes were surrounded by the small lines which come from too much laughing. Rose and Adelle saw her through the glass doors, and both knew at once that this would be good vacation. Adelle knocked and Pat, who was on the phone, opened the door, took Adelle's hand saying, "You must be Adelle, June fifth through June ninth. Be with you in a jiff."

Adelle stood, Pat holding her hand as she finished up her phone conversation, and looked at peace. Rose was glad. She had forgotten how long it had been since she had seen that look on Adelle's face.

Pat finally got off the phone, hugged them both effusively, and showed them the suite. It was perfect — all pink and lacy with a few many-paned windows which looked off into the deepness of the blue-green patterned waters. The breeze pushed the laciness of the curtains into the room, and the air smelled like freshly salted watermelon.

As Adelle brought up their things, Rose made a small tray of snacks, mostly fresh fruit and cheese. Then she made them each a wine cooler with crushed mint leaves and shaved ice.

They sat out on the veranda which was off the small kitchen, and Adelle, feeling happy, ate everything on the plate in a matter of moments.

"How do you do this, prepare these instant feasts?"

"Planning. And getting you to carry up everything." Rose smiled. It only took a small compliment to get her mind in gear. For dinner she would make the flank steak stuffed with spinach and pine nuts, a salad of artichoke hearts on a bed of romaine lettuce with her own famed blue cheese and crushed pecan dressing, and a light-as-air cheese souffle.

"I've got to pick up a few things at the grocery store, Adelle. Want to come for a walk?"

"I thought you bought all of Fairfax. Wasn't that enough? Now do you have to buy out Mendocino? Your shopping habits are causing food shortages all up and down the coast."

"We can get an ice cream cone on the way. I saw a place coming in."

Off they went.

* * * * *

They spent the days and nights in glorious peaceful pleasure. They buried themselves in clean sheets and let the smell of the ocean tumble over them. They ate Pat's home-baked pastries, which she left at the door each morning, and drank rich dark coffee. They walked the beach, being brave enough when they were alone to hold hands, strong against the winds from the sea.

Rose made some of the most glorious meals she had ever made, and Adelle ate with the fervor they deserved. They tried a restaurant once but it wasn't as nice as their little place, and the food wasn't as good as Rose's. Walking home from the restaurant, it seemed so good, as if all they needed on earth was each other.

"Will you still love me?"

Rose brushed against Adelle for an instant, in a manner no one would take for sensual, though it was. "We've been through a lot together, you and I." Adelle sighed.

Their last night at Pat's, the air was warm and still. They sat on the veranda, their chairs touching. Rose had, earlier in the day, hollowed out the middle of a small watermelon, and poured a bit of creme de menthe, a cup and a half of Tanqueray gin, a cup of rhine wine, and a cup of pineapple juice. It had been mellowing all day, cooling in the refrigerator. Now they sipped the chilled liquid out through straws set in two small holes Rose had made. They took turns holding the cold green melon.

On the small wrought iron table in front of them were small shish ka-bobs of baked scallops, water chestnuts, green and red peppers, and shrimp, with a spicy cajun sauce for dipping.

By the time the moon lay like silk across the ocean, they were in bed, wrapped around each other, smelling of pepper and fruit and the finest of liquors.

* * * * *

Rose took Adelle to the hospital exactly at noon. During the drive, Adelle gave Rose endless instructions. "Water the plants tomorrow. The succulents get a drop of plant food, the others just

108

plain water. If I get any mail, bring it to me. If anyone calls while I'm in the hospital, you may tell them where I am generally, in other words, in the hospital, but don't give them my number. Unless, that is, they're on the list of people I will talk to, which I gave you last night. Remember where you put it? Right next to the phone."

She babbled on about small things until they got to the bridge. Coming from Marin to San Francisco was often like entering a dark cave without a flashlight. The devouring fog which swept across the bridge seemed to remove the color from the day, turning the sun of the suburbs into the grey gloom of the city. As soon as they hit the first wall of fog, Adelle stopped talking, and the only sound, aside from the click of the wheels against the metal strips of the road, was the lonely sounding violin music coming from the radio.

* * * * *

The hospital room was small and compact with Jesus on the cross next to the bathroom door. He was silver. Adelle had brought along her briefcase crammed with work. It had more items in it than her small overnight bag did.

They hugged goodbye, and leaving was one of the hardest things Rose had ever done. But the operation would be tomorrow, and Adelle needed to sleep.

Rose called when she got home to the endlessly empty house. "Hi." She tried to sound happy.

"Oh. Hello."

"I love you."

"I love you too."

109

There was nothing more to say.

Rose stayed up until midnight. She watered the plants, and fed the succulents. She walked the dog four times. She thought of calling Evan, to ask him to send flowers, but then she recalled that he didn't even know Adelle was being operated on. All he knew was that she had cancer. She called her own mother, thinking her mother might be supportive. Her mother said, "Good. I don't give a damn if she dies or not." Rose hung up.

The operation was scheduled for nine-thirty, and Rose was there by eight. She had brought Adelle some bagels from David's, and a bouquet of flowers, all lavender and pink. She also brought along a book on the Australian aborigines to read while she waited.

Adelle was in bed, wearing a flowered hospital gown, an IV tube plunged into her left hand. The nurse's name was Randal, and he had a small Charlie Chaplin-type moustache. As he busied himself with Adelle, he chatted to Rose, saying that he had just passed his State Boards. The intern was a young woman with glasses larger than her smile. Her name was Janice.

As they rolled Adelle onto the gurney, she said, heavy with the drugs they had dripped into her, "I'm in love with Janice."

Rose walked along the corridor as they pushed the gurney. She held Adelle's hand. It was allowable under such circumstances. "I thought you were in love with your surgeon."

"That was last week. Today I love Janice." Randal kept a stiff upper moustache. He parked the gurney in the huge square elevator, and gave Rose a hug, whispering, "She'll be all right. She'll be fine.

Why not give her a kiss? For luck." Rose kissed
Adelle softly, and the doors swept shut, leaving her in
the long beige hallway.

She went back to the room to wait. They were
going to do a two-part operation. First under the
arms to see if the nodes were positive. If they were,
Adelle would have a mastectomy. If they weren't, she
would have a lumpectomy. The surgeon had promised
to call Rose in the room as soon as they had
examined the nodes.

She sat back with Jesus behind her, and read the
book. It said that the aborigine male, to become an
adult, has an incisor tooth knocked out with a rock.
Then he had his penis slit from stem to stern. The
author said there was much beauty in the ceremony.
The author, a male, said that knowledge was of more
value in cultures without a written language, and
that calculators had made memorizing the timetables
obsolete. Rose knew, though, that at times batteries
died or electricity failed, and the seven timetables
would always be a pisser if one had to rely on
oneself.

The surgeon rang at noon. "The nodes seem to be
negative. We're feeling very hopeful and lucky. There
were a few enlarged ones, but that might be the
result of the biop. She's resting now and should be
back to her room in a few hours. You're welcome."
Rose had not said thank you.

She returned to the aborigine book. Aborigines
disliked flying biting insects as much as the white
Australians did. She put the book down. It had
seemed like forever between the first suspicion and
today, but it had really only been a few weeks. Most
women would have acted more quickly, would have

had an operation the same day if they could. But Adelle needed to be sure, needed to be sure about everything in her life. For her, there was safety in certainty. She never could grasp that certainty didn't exist.

Rose had never read so many books about a single subject in so short a time, except maybe anthropology or philosophy. Who could have known that in an operation for breast cancer, the most painful and most debilitating part was an operation on the nodes under one's arms? If the nodes were negative as the doctor seemed to believe, the lumpectomy itself would be a much simpler operation. Adelle would have it in the morning, and be home by early evening. Another wait as the lab checked the nodes. But at least Adelle would be home with Rose, home where Rose could make her safe. She looked over her shoulder at Jesus. She hadn't realized until that moment that he was made of plastic covered with a shiny silver. It was a small chip which gave him away, showed the dull colored material underneath.

They wheeled Adelle back in at two. She was sleeping.

* * * * *

A while later, someone came in to take her blood pressure. She awoke, licked her lips, and sleepily asked, "What's the pressure?"

The nurse went on trying to get a reading. "Don't you worry about it, Adelle honey. We'll take care of everything."

Adelle persisted, sounding annoyed through her sleepiness. "What is it? And don't call me honey."

"Ninety over seventy."

"Too low," Adelle muttered, and fell back asleep.

The nurse unhooked the apparatus from around Adelle's arm. "You just rest," he whispered.

Randal left, and Rose touched Adelle's hand. "I'm here, Adelle."

Rose stayed while Adelle slept, wanting to be there when she awakened. She read that Australia had more types of snakes than any other continent; it even had cobras. Adelle would moan now and then. Rose would touch her hair. "I'm here, Adelle."

Adelle always answered. "Good, Sweetie, good," even if she didn't open her eyes.

Randal finally came in and told Rose that she would have to leave, that it was past visiting hours. He said Adelle would sleep through the night. "And don't worry. I'm here. I'll be watching out for her."

Rose left, feeling good until she was halfway home and realized that Randal's shift would be over soon. He had been there since she'd gotten there in the morning.

For dinner Rose ate half a pound of raw ground chuck, topped with some chopped onions and green peppers. It was the only thing that sounded good to her stomach. On TV, the Grand Ol' Opry was celebrating its sixtieth birthday. Dolly Parton sang "Coat of Many Colors," and Rose cried. Dolly's mother came on and said that the story in the song was a true one. Rose cried even harder.

* * * * *

Rose was at the hospital by seven. She had a fresh cheese Danish, some blueberries, a small carton

113

of cream, and another bouquet of flowers. She and Randal arrived at the door at the same time, though coming from opposite directions. "Well, you're here bright and early, or did you spend the night?"

Adelle looked up from her bed, piled high with work, to study the traffic jam at her door. She smiled. "Well, good morning. I'm starving!"

Randal laughed. "That's a good sign." He did not know that Adelle could eat seventy dollars worth of groceries in the space of an hour and still feel hungry. He set up Adelle's breakfast tray, fitting it neatly over the papers spread out on the covers. Rose sat down and watched as an orderly brought in the breakfast on a cart: a piece of white toasted bread, plain, a container of orange juice, coffee, and a poached egg in a white plastic container. The tray was also white, as were the napkin and the plastic utensils.

In seventh grade, during the only cooking class she ever took, Rose had seen a film featuring Alan Ladd before he was a star. He was demonstrating how to correctly carve the roast beef. A male voice, not his, gave a stern warning to the future homemakers of America: "And, of course, *never* serve food on a blue plate." Rose, not being one to accept advice easily, had never bought a plate in a color other than blue since then. Looking at the sad little white egg in its white basket on its white tray, she knew again how wrong that film had been. The egg would have looked great on blue. On white it looked like a pigeon splash on cement.

Adelle, not one to be much bothered by the lack of beauty, gulped down the egg, toast, and the orange

114

juice. Then she looked at Rose. "Good to see you, Sweetie. Did you bring me a little snack?"

Rose gave her the Danish, rinsed out the egg basket and filled it with berries and cream. Adelle was just finishing off the last bite of Danish, which she had dunked into the cup of coffee Rose had gotten from the machine down the hall, when a large group of interns came in, clipboards in hand.

"How are we doing? Have we managed to eat anything yet?"

Adelle wiped her mouth with the paper napkin. "I've managed a little something."

"We were worried about your low blood pressure yesterday, but it looks good now. Keep up the good work."

They left, and Rose laughed. "Even while escaping the clutches of death, food is a priority."

"Thanks, Sweetie. It made it feel like home."

They were silent for a while, holding hands.

"I would prefer you not die, Adelle; I really would prefer that."

"I would prefer that also. I would like to live a long time, as long as the quality of my life is pleasant."

"How scared are you?"

"I'm scared shitless."

For some reason, that made Rose very happy. It made sense to be scared, especially in the hospital. The rain looked noisy, though they couldn't hear it through the double-paned hermetically sealed window.

They shared the paper, Adelle taking the business section, Rose the rest. "Listen to this, Adelle. Seems it is now possible for males to give birth to children."

She read Adelle parts of the article and showed her the cartoon of a pregnant male. " 'The egg would be fertilized, then placed in the abdomen of the male parent, where it would grow either next to the kidney or in the small intestine.' " Rose closed the paper. "Whatever do you think of that?"

"What's the point?"

"You know how men are. A challenge, I guess. Still, I wonder, if your father is your mother, would you call him mother, and, if so, would you call your mother father?"

They sat and tried to think why a man would want to take on a woman's role in the creation process. Would an aborigine male want to be a mother if he could, or would he rather bash his teeth out and slice his penis to pieces?

Finally Adelle answered the question. "I think they would still call him father, because an intestine is not a womb."

That made sense to Rose.

* * * * *

The next day, Rose arrived later, but spent the entire day. Except for the IV tree, it was hard to tell Adelle had undergone any trauma. As soon as Rose entered the room, Adelle beamed. "What, may I ask, do you have in that large bag?"

"Close your eyes, Adelle, and don't open them until I tell you to." Adelle pretended to, though Rose knew she was peeking. After a while she said, "Okay. Open." There, lined up on the bureau, was what seemed to be the entire front display cabinet of a New York deli. There, all wrapped in Saran Wrap, was a pastrami sandwich on rye with mustard, mayo and lettuce, and a carton of coleslaw, both from David's. From the bakery was a chocolate eclair, a half a cheesecake with fresh strawberry topping, and a pineapple Danish. And, from Rose's own kitchen, made last night by the light of the moon, was a boned whole chicken, stuffed with white raisins, crushed Brazil nuts, and garlic made mild by baking it until it was soft and gently pungent. The crust of the chicken was a rich russet color, having been basted every fifteen minutes with a coat of honey, wine, and ginger. And, of course to go with it, fresh asparagus vinaigrette.

Adelle gasped softly, then recovered. "What? No ice cream?"

Just then Randal walked in with Adelle's mid-morning snack: a small cup of canned mixed fruit and an oatmeal cookie. They all laughed as he looked at the bureau and its treasures.

The day went by slowly, almost drip by drip. Interns came and went, checking this and that. Adelle read, worked, and ate. Rose read, watched Adelle eat, and every hour or so took a long walk down the halls to stretch her legs.

Night came softly. The birds slowly shut down. The trees went from substance to shadow. Looking out the window, it was as if one had dropped a bit of India ink into a glass of clear water. The darkness began to cover the clearness, but the eye couldn't catch the change.

With most of the food gone, and it almost time for Rose to leave, she and Adelle went down to the hospital chapel. It was dark and deep with stained-glass men in robes seeming to walk around the entire perimeter. The altar had a small sad sign on it: PLEASE PRAY FOR THOSE PEOPLE WHO DIED IN THE MONTH OF JUNE. There was a long list of names. Adelle, wearing her flowered hospital gown with a sweater thrown over it, pushed her IV tree in front of her, looking at the stained glass men. Then she burped. It was a loud life-affirming burp to be heard by the robed men all over the world. The noise clung to the chapel, refusing to be ignored.

"Do you think anyone heard?" Adelle asked, pulling the sweater tightly around, her neck red for the second time Rose could remember.

"I heard it, Adelle. And the men walking around the ceiling. I'm glad I heard it. Don't you see? It means you're alive; you're okay. It was incredibly healthy."

* * * * *

Rose got to the hospital at seven, and Adelle was all ready to go. She looked the same as she had when she checked in three days ago except for a small drain in the pocket of her blouse. Its purpose was to collect the fluids, mostly blood, which would build up in her armpit area. When Adelle took it out and showed it to her, Rose thought it looked a bit like E.T.'s heart line.

They checked out, making certain to say goodbye to Randal, to thank him for his special care, and headed for home. The bridge was heavy with traffic, but most of it was going the other way. This time they went from the fog into the sun. Marin County burst forth like the sun on the flag of Japan. Without knowing why, they both breathed a deep

118

sigh. On the bay far below, sails of many colors moved slowly, leaned against the wind. Adelle rolled down her window, breathing deeply. "I've been breathing canned air for days. God that smells good, Rose. Who invented windows which can't open?"

"I don't know." Rose made a note to herself to look that up.

The air poured in. "Rose. I want you to know that I love you."

"Because I'm a good cook?"

"Because you are there, across the table, across the road, across the bed. There. Always there, just a heartbeat away."

"We'll be okay, Adelle. You'll be fine."

"Always there."

Adelle slept late her first night home. By nine o'clock Rose was beginning to get scared. She was not sure what to do if someone died. By ten she decided to wake her up. She went and sat on the floor by the bed, and said her name softly. "Adelle. Turn on your heart line."

Adelle flashed alive, causing some of the pale pink fluid to splash against the wall. "Today I'm going to clean the entire house. The clutter is driving me mad, just mad." She pulled at her nose and looked serious.

Rose wondered why she had bothered to awaken her.

It was a bit of a problem for Adelle to take a shower since there was nothing to attach her drain to. Finally Rose stood in the water with her, holding it, although Adelle always had the water about twenty degrees above tolerable in Rose's opinion. She helped Adelle dress, and began to help her down the stairs. Adelle pulled away. "I can do it." Even if she hadn't heard the phone call last night, Rose would have known it. All the signs were there. Evan was coming.

* * * * *

Adelle spent the whole day cleaning house. She watered plants, vacuumed, swept, rubbed, waxed, ironed, and rearranged. She was a frenzy of energy.

Knowing that her help would be spurned, Rose sat and played solitaire. She couldn't even cook since Evan had said he would stop at Fisherman's Wharf and get a couple of steamed crabs, some French bread, and make a salad from the vegetables he had grown in his garden.

Rose would get Adelle glasses of ice water, would carry the vacuum cleaner from room to room, would sing the work song from *Snow White,* but mostly would stay out of the way. Adelle would talk now and then, make small comments which Rose did not feel were directed at her, and to which she made no reply.

"He's pretty shitty, isn't he? Sort of self-centered and into his own thing." Work, rub, scrub. "I don't think he really knows or cares what this cancer thing has done to me." Work, rub, scrub. "He might love himself too much or too little to really love anyone else." Work, scrub, rub. "Heck, Rose. Are you listening? I said I know Evan loves me. He most certainly does. He's getting a couple of crabs, just for me." Adelle sat down with a plop, and looked totally exhausted. She fell into a deep sleep in the chair. Rose took the rag out of her hand, put a pillow behind her head, and covered her with a light blanket.

Even though it was Adelle who had done all the work, Rose felt exhausted. She also felt like crying, though she wasn't sure why. The soliloquy from *Carousel* kept running through her head. She ordinarily would have sung it aloud, but she didn't want to wake Adelle.

It was dark when Evan barrelled in, and Adelle had just awakened. He started talking and grabbing the moment he walked though the door, not bothering to knock.

"Well, this place is a son of a bitch to find, a real son of a bitch." He hugged Adelle, who winced in pain. He looked at Rose and decided not to hug her. Sometimes he did; sometimes he didn't. "And this poor old body ain't what it used to be back when." He stretched and massaged his lower back area. "Now I gotta have me a beer. One of them ice-cold Millers." He opened the cooler he had carted in with him, and popped open a beer, and, holding the can a few inches above his face, he poured a stream into his mouth. Some of it splashed onto the floor Adelle had just cleaned. "Mmmmmm. I tell you. There is times when there ain't nothing as fine as a beer. Sometimes even beats having a woman. Not often mind you, but at times." He sat down in the chair Rose always sat in, the one which faced the pond. "Like this here place. Yes I do. Purdy. Real purdy. Nice pond out there."

"Evan. Did you bring the crabs?" Adelle sounded worried.

"Hell yes. Did I bring the crabs: got three big

121

ones. One for me, and two for my baby. Hell, them suckers are getting to cost more than a trip to the whorehouse. Rose, get that table set up so me and my baby girl can eat us a meal."

Rose was used to Evan, and kept her cool. She made a sauce with fresh lemon juice, Tabasco, horseradish, and ketchup, sliced some lemons, and got out the blue plates. "Ready."

Evan pulled out a chair for Adelle, sat down, and looked at the lemons and the sauce. "Old lady's food. Makes your lips pucker and your gift to women droop. Hell and hell's fire. I like to taste my crab meat murky and pure. Now come on honey, let's dig in." They all ate, although Rose felt like a third wheel. Then, with the crab shells empty and the French bread just a few pieces of crust, Adelle took a small sip of beer. "So, Evan, what's your latest girl friend like? Is she younger than me?"

Evan took a sip of his tenth beer. "Nope. A bit older. Fifty-one last week." He winked. "You wouldn't want me to be lonely, would you?"

"And what is the status of your illegitimate children?"

It was something they always went through, as much a part of their relationship as the crabs Evan always brought when he came to visit, wherever Rose and Adelle were living.

"See them now and then, those I know of. All smart as a whip, with hair blonde enough to be sunbeams."

"And how does Ann handle all this?"

"Ann and I," said Evan, retelling the story for the millionth time it seemed to Rose, "had a fine relationship until I married her. Then all hell broke loose and the bottom fell out. Man marries a woman and the money he's got is up for grabs. She don't see him, she sees his pants pocket. I don't wish her ill, and she can have what's left when I take the final ride, but I tell you, it is pure hell to wake up and see her face there, right alongside the sun."

Adelle's heart line was getting filled. "I would like to ask, as your only living legitimate heir, that you will me some of your assets when you die."

Rose, though she heard it all so often, always wondered what they were really talking about. Adelle, Rose knew, had left much of her money for Evan's care, should he fall ill and be unable to care for himself. He never would say whom he left his to. Rose usually decided it was their own little language of love.

Evan was planning to stay at least until Monday when the results of Adelle's lymph nodes would be known. "Might stay longer. Depends how my darling needs me to care for her." He kissed the top of her head. "Don't worry, baby. Daddy's here to take care of you."

As they all went to bed, Sunday tucked itself safely away, and Monday loomed large in Rose's future. "Night, Evan." "Night, Adelle." "Night, John Boy."

* * * * *

Adelle slept late, leaving Rose to face Evan and the morning alone. Rose made coffee, got the paper, and ate a peach. She had bought Evan some Kellogg's Bran Flakes, which had been his favorite, and had gotten Adelle her usual morning apple fritter. Laden

123

with her gifts, she waited for the world to awaken. As she was reading about the new emergence of white supremacy groups on the rise in California, Evan thundered down the stairs, his words filling the lovely morning with noise.

"I can see you thought it would please me if you made me a pot of brew, but I'm here to tell you, face to face, that I make the best damned java in the world, and prefer making my own." He reached over and hugged Rose with his arms around her neck. "Just kidding girl. You know that. Hell, a man with my sexual energies needs to stay awake. Some little filly might be in need." He sat in Adelle's seat, and began to read the paper, glasses low on his nose.

"I think I'll take the dog for a walk."

He looked up. "Damned good idea. That mutt's way too fat. Like to bust from excess calories. Feed her once a day. She don't eat it, you take it up. Keep it down all the time like you do, and she nibbles all day, just like some pampered housewife. Shit, you don't know much about dogs, do you?"

Rose walked out into the coolness of the morning, and walked as long as she could. Actually, she would have stayed out all day, but she was worried about Adelle. When she returned, Evan was now in her seat, drinking coffee, and studying the sports page. He looked over the edge of the paper as she and Dollars came in.

"Coffee ain't too bad. I'm gonna wait on my cereal till my baby gets herself up. You can take the sea bass out of the freezer. I put them there last night. Cook 'em up one of them fancy ways you know. And use some of the zucchini I brung. Make a salad if you like. Ever do that, put zucchini in salads?"

Rose nodded yes, and started upstairs to see about Adelle.

"You always have that painful music on? Sounds like some form of Chinese torture, where they drop water on your head till you pee your pants and forget where a woman's point of entry is."

Rose turned off the harpsichord music and decided that she would have a strong drink as soon as it was ethically possible. Just then Adelle came down, looking pale and tired. Rose poured her a cup of coffee, and rubbed her neck as she sat drinking it.

"Well, Evan," Adelle asked, ignoring Rose. "Did you sleep well?"

Evan jumped up and squeezed Adelle's arm, unable to get nearer since Rose was still massaging her neck. "My daughter. My number one daughter. Just tell me what you want. Let me know, and I'll get it for you, baby."

Rose took the fritter out of the microwave, and put it on a plate in front of Adelle. "I just want breakfast right now, Evan. Rose just gave it to me."

"Did you sleep well, baby? You're the sick one. I'm only here to help. Did you sleep well?"

"I had some pain last night. Actually, an amazing amount."

"Course you did. Course. Look at the rabbit out there, eating just the tips of them berry plants. Ain't that something?"

Rose Penski slipped into her own mind as the talk turned to money. As Evan and Adelle talked about *his* fifty thousand dollar investment, *her* refinancing an apartment, *his* sale of the river cabin, *her* latest sale, Rose thought about the various ways it was possible to poison a person without being detected or suspected. Oleander tea, hillside mushrooms chosen at random, a can of soup, hole poked in its side, left to bulge with poison until serving time. Suddenly Evan was standing, stretching his arms towards the ceiling. "Well," and his words eased out as slowly as cold honey. "Let's get started. Big high-powered broad like you, must be messages piled to the ceiling. Bet them sales people of yours just hang on your every word. Let's haul ass, daughter. You're your daddy's little girl. There's money to be made."

Adelle focused on a point in the room not evident to others and said, "Well, now that you mention it, yes, I suppose I should be getting back to the office. Why don't you shower and shave. I've got to gather up some things. We can spend some time together at my office."

They scurried off. Rose began to clean up after breakfast, although Evan had rinsed his own cup. Adelle went upstairs and made some phone calls. Evan walked outside to see if he could figure where the points of the compass were. He called, "Rose, get your butt out here." Rose went, knowing that to make a fuss was pointless.

"Where the hell is east? Can't tell where the sun is for all these damned trees."

"Right there, Evan, where the wild canary is, in the juniper tree."

"Can't be. Don't make no sense."

Just then Adelle called out the window from upstairs. "Rose. Come here. Now. I need you."

Evan ignored the urgency in the voice, and stared at the sun, shielding his eyes from the rays.

Rose bounded upstairs two at a time, jumping over the dog which was halfway between floors claiming a patch of sun that hit the house early and made dance patterns on the orchid-colored rug. "What's wrong, Adelle?" She was scared. Adelle was sitting on the toilet.

"I can't poop," Adelle moaned. "It's been five days. My stomach feels like it's filled with rocks. They said this might happen. I think you have to get me a Fleet Enema. Should I write that down?"

Rose was off in a flash, Evan yelling after her as her car careened down the hill: "Don't be going to the God damned store. Ain't a damned thing we need. Hell, ain't even room for my beer in the refrigerator. You shop too much, like some crazy dingbat —"

By the time Rose got to the mailbox at the foot of the driveway, he had either stopped, or she could no longer hear him.

* * * * *

Adelle and Evan stayed at the office for several hours, and Rose Penski used the time to great advantage. She went to the edge of the hill on which they lived, and sang the angry songs from *West Side Story*. She had the strong drink she had promised herself, a mixture of one hundred proof rum, freshly squeezed mango pulp, and yogurt. She squeezed the three mangoes she used by hand, the pit slipping free often as she tightened her palms around it. It was a drink she had invented on the spot, and it was so good she had another. She thought about putting Evan's beers out in the sun to heat, and popping them back in when she heard the car drive up, but she decided that was sick. Sick, but she still liked the idea. The hospital was to call sometime after five to report on Adelle's nodes. It would be a long afternoon.

Evan and Adelle came back in time for lunch, then Adelle went upstairs to take a nap (something she never did unless Evan came to visit), and Evan took a lounge chair out by a pond to work on his suntan. He fell asleep with his socks on, a white handkerchief over his face to protect his nose. Rose thought he would have an odd pattern of tan, and went to reading more about the aborigines. Evan awakened only once, sweat dripping from his body. He looked over at Rose. "Risky to sit by an old coot like me when the sun is warming my body parts." Then he went back to sleep.

You don't scare me, you old fool, Rose thought, and went back to her book. The book said that aborigines are more religious than Catholics. Evan was Catholic, or so he said. Catholicism has a lot of self-imposed problems, Rose thought. Most men seemed to feel that if they didn't have sex, they were as good as dead. Rose often wondered what the Pope did with his sex. Evan talked it to death, then dozed off into the handkerchiefed safety of the sun. Mahatma Ghandi used to have a young virgin sleep next to him as a test of his own purity.

Rose's book said that when religion lost its magic, it died. Only the unknown keeps life in the living. At this point in time, in the lives of Rose and Adelle, the unknown certainly had power. In a few hours the phone would ring, and upon it would rest two futures. Rose sat, a few flies buzzing around her head, and took a bite of the apple she had brought out with her. Yes, cancer was a god. It controlled life: it gave and took. It was a mystery rolled in the vacant memory of clouds. She took another bite, swished at the flies, and turned the page. The aborigines believed they were born of kangaroos.

* * * * *

The phone call came a few moments before six. The nodes were negative; Adelle did not have spreading cancer. This meant she could have the lumpectomy. It increased her long-term chances of survival. It was damned good news.

Rose went downstairs, tears building at the corners of her eyes. She felt so good she even gave Evan a big hug. "She's going to be okay, Evan, she's going to be okay."

They stood quietly hugging each other for a moment, and then Evan broke away and did the old man *Zorba the Greek* dance, kicking at imaginary sands with his toes, flinging his arms about as though to knock down all the walls of the world.

Adelle came down slowly, and sat at the table. She folded her hands, and looked up at the others. "I guess we can assume that the news is good. The lab reports have been reliably read, and my survival chances are a bit higher as of today."

They all decided to take the dog for her walk, Evan babbling the whole way like some demented remnant of a Jewish mother. "Now, don't be walking too fast. Don't be going too far. Watch out for them

129

there rocks on the side. Don't get over-tired. Keep your pace down."

Now that it was clear that Adelle would probably get better, not die right off the bat, he began to fret and worry. Rose saw a long week looming ahead. "Watch them branches overhead, baby. Take care."

Suddenly Rose surprised herself by shouting, "Oh shut up you old bag of wind."

Evan smiled and slipped his arm around her waist. "Gladly darling. I love a fiery woman."

* * * * *

The next day, again, everyone slept late. Rose finally got up about eight, though there seemed to be some tiredness still clinging to her bones. As she had her cup of morning coffee, it was one of the few times in her life she felt she actually *needed* it. Perhaps, she thought to herself, good news is just as exhausting as bad news. That was too depressing to contemplate so she decided to count her blessings. She was up to blessing number two when Evan came downstairs.

He pointed to her cup of coffee. "Give me some of that, and don't be such a damned hog about the paper. Lord, women ain't worth much if you let 'em have any power."

Rose had spent too many hours with Evan, and she wanted only meat for breakfast. She somehow thought that eating like a beast would make her more able to cope. As she was planning what to fix, Evan looked up from the paper. "I'll take some of that melon in the refrigerator." Rose decided to fast, giving up the idea that eating meat would be of

130

value. This required sainthood, not ferocity. She got Evan his melon, and set it on the table in front of him. Her plan was to drink only distilled water at room temperature until he left. She was just filling up her glass when he spoke again. Like Adelle, he often spoke with food in his mouth. "Could you warm up that apple fritter setting on the counter there? These old bones are craving sugar, and when my body gets a craving, I give it satisfaction."

Rose thought maybe, to go along with her fast, she would begin to wear thorns in her sandals, or perhaps go without her glasses. As she gave him the apple fritter, he held up his coffee cup. "You know you put a speck too many spoons of coffee in that pot. Gives it too much of a bite. Ought to wash it out now and then too."

A glorious silence reigned as Evan read the sports section of the paper. Rose could even hear the birds. It was just like old times. Then Adelle came down, said hello, and asked if Rose could heat up the apple fritter. Adelle always had breakfast on her mind the moment she entered the kitchen in the morning.

"Evan is eating it. I have some blueberry Danish though."

Adelle looked hurt. "I had my taste buds set on an apple fritter."

Evan threw the paper down. "Hell, if my baby wants an apple fritter, I'll go out and get her a God damned apple fritter. Where do you get these things, Rose, and why the hell didn't you tell me Adelle'd want one for breakfast? How'm I supposed to know these women things?"

Rose gave him instructions. It wasn't far to the bakery, and he left wearing a pair of plaid walking

131

shorts, a sleeveless white undershirt, and slippers. As he slammed the door behind him, the delightful silence of earlier returned.

Rose and Adelle sat at the table. Adelle was softly hitting the side of her coffee cup with her spoon. Finally she spoke. "He is a bit much to take, isn't he?"

Rose Penski knew that this was a time for total silence. It was a rare occasion indeed when Adelle said even the slightest thing of a negative nature about Evan to Rose. Had Rose taken the bait, had she agreed, had she stood up, turned cartwheels, screamed, yelled and shouted, "Yes, the old fool is as hard to take as sitting in a bathtub filled with snakes, spiders, and slugs," then, at some time in the future, when she and Adelle were arguing about something, anything — it wouldn't matter what — Adelle would say, winning the battle hands down, "You never did like Evan either. You were always saying he was a bit much to take."

So it was, with wisdom and restraint, that Rose replied only in her head, turning cartwheels, screaming, yelling, shouting, "Yes, the old fool is as hard to take as sitting in a tub filled with slimey hairy things that no one can tolerate." What Adelle saw of all of this was a slight shrug of the shoulders.

* * * * *

The night before the lumpectomy, Rose made a special dinner, which, happily, kept her in the kitchen much of the day and out of the range of Evan. Except at mealtime, he called the kitchen the woman's place. Rose baked, and stuffed, and carved,

132

and blended. Now and then Adelle would walk by, and say, "My, my. Smells good." Evan would come in for a beer, belch or make some inane comment, then go back out to the lounge chair. Adelle and Evan were outside, talking, as Rose worked. Rose knew they only had a few conversations, all of which they repeated each time they got together. It had been that way for years. Once Adelle, over the phone, had shouted at Evan, "Evan, this isn't the same old conversation. I'm trying to *tell* you something." Rose figured by now they were onto the exchange about whether Adelle's mother was truly ill, or just bad.

Rose's final result was the triumph she hoped it would be. The huge oriental melon had been hollowed out and stuffed with a mixture of lobster tail chunks, shiitake mushrooms, sake, and Monterey Jack cheese. The outer rind had been lovingly carved with the message SAPPHO WAS A RIGHT ON WOMAN, with small nymphs dancing around the words. Rose knew that Evan wouldn't get the message, so it was a secret I love you which the two women could share in spite of him. Just before it was served, she would bake it long enough for the cheese to melt to the bubbling point, and the sake to turn to fumes of flavor in the lobster chunks. To go with it Rose was serving a broccoli salad with mustard sauce, sticky rice, and cucumbers stuffed with crab, green onion tips, and shredded red peppers.

She went out and got a film for the VCR which she hoped would be pure escapism, a science fiction one called *Dune,* and then she went to sit with Evan and Adelle for a while before the sun grew chilly. Rose had figured it right, they were on the conversation about Adelle's mother. Had either of them left for a moment, Rose could have filled in, as she knew all the questions, all the answers, by heart. She sat on the outskirts of their conversation, a part of it for certain, but not a participant.

* * * * *

The dinner was a success, although Adelle had a few too many drinks, something she rarely did, and the movie was just the usual male nonsense about a Christ figure undergoing challenges to see if he was the chosen one. Also, a lot of the violence was difficult to stomach. Evan seemed to like it, although he kept saying he didn't get what it was all about.

After the movie, Rose and Adelle excused themselves. Evan said he'd stay downstairs for a while, just relax a bit and watch the news. Both women knew that he waited until he thought they were asleep, then made phone calls to his girl friends in Bakersfield, telling them how he was being such a help to his baby.

It had only been five days since Adelle's lymph nodes operation, and she still wore her drain, though she didn't have to empty it quite as often. She and Rose hadn't slept in the same bed because the slightest move could cause great pain. Rose slept on a small rollaway cot next to the big bed.

Adelle looked at Rose, the alcohol making her face look a bit like it did when she was angry, making her eyes, usually so soft, look hard and stern.

"Is it helpful, Sweetie, for you to have him here? I asked him just to help you out."

Now Rose Penski was no fool, and she was not about to engage in a debate regarding motives. A good motto in life, she had learned, was when in doubt, use a non-sequitur. So she replied, good-naturedly, "You seem to be enjoying him."

Alcohol did not sharpen Adelle's brains any more than it did anyone else's, but it stripped away her veneer of obliviousness. "Rose. Be honest. Is Evan making it easier for you?" She hiccupped. "That's the only reason I asked him."

Rose had to make a quick choice. She could be honest, or she could lie. Adelle would know if she lied, which was why she was asking the question. On the other hand, the chances were good that Adelle would not recall Rose's response, whatever it was. Rose opted for honesty.

"Well, the truth is, he tells loud anti-woman jokes until early afternoon, when he passes out from his beers. He wakes up in time for a few beers before dinner, tells some more jokes, eats, makes phone calls, and goes to bed."

"I knew it. He's not much comfort."

They were silent for a moment. Rose, encouraged by the peaceful acceptance of her reply, went on.

"Also, Adelle, he is peeing all over the downstairs bathroom. There are splatter marks on the wall and floor. I've seen bad aim, but his is non-existent. It's beginning to stink. I know he doesn't do dishes, let alone bathrooms, and I can't ask you, in your condition to do it. So, on top of it all, I'm going to have to clean up his piss when he leaves. I'm not sure why there are men in this world."

Rose had gotten a bit more carried away than she had planned to, and the power in her voice had wiped away a bit of Adelle's fogginess. It had been a dangerous gambit, and Rose bit her tongue.

"Well," said Adelle, in a most forgiving manner, "he's getting old."

Rose climbed into her cot, trying to come up with a saving remark. Just before Adelle started snoring, it came to her. "Adelle. You know, it *is* nice to have someone to carry out the garbage."

* * * * *

The lumpectomy was to be an out-patient procedure, provided all went well. Adelle would be in at ten, and out by six. Rose had wisely bought three apple fritters, so breakfast went smoothly. Adelle, although she was facing her third bodily assault in less than a month, seemed in good spirits.

"I hope Randal is there again, Rose. I really liked him."

"I thought you were in love with Janice, the M.D."

Adelle smiled. "Oh thanks, Sweetie. I had forgotten she would be there too. This is going to be a good day."

Rose felt a tightening of the spine. It was not like Adelle to take things so calmly. The phone rang. It was for Adelle. It was a Mr. Wang, and she took it upstairs.

When she finally came down, she looked like a wild animal hearing the first shot of hunting season. She brushed by Rose and went into the study. "I've got to get a letter off to Mr. Wang right away. It has to be in the mail within the next hour."

Rose felt anger shaking most parts of her body. "Adelle," she said quite loudly, "you have to leave for the hospital in less than thirty minutes. Mr. Wang can wait. He can just God damned wait."

Adelle looked as if she were walking through the gates of hell. Her skin was white, and her eyes looked like chocolate frosting smudges on a wedding gown of white lace. Her lips, which she had already rouged, were vampire-red against the paleness of her skin.

"Rose." Adelle was packing up bits of this and that to ship off to Mr. Wang. "You are a child about finances. Mr. Wang needs these materials right away. Now!"

"I don't give a hell of a sailor's butt if you have a million deals to close before you go. Adelle, you are programming yourself to destruction. You should be relaxing, thinking languid waterfall thoughts, and deep breathing. Instead you are running around like the fool you have been all your life, thinking that if you do something which seems important enough, like mail things to Mr. Wang, you will be cured of cancer. Stop it!"

Adelle sat at the typewriter in obvious pain, coddling her right breast. "I would appreciate it if you would not holler at me. Evan can take me to the post office to mail this if you are in one of your moods."

"Post office? You are *not* going to the post office, you escapee from the loony bin. You're going to the hospital for an operation on your cancerous growth."

Rose knew, the way that mountains know when a storm is coming, that Adelle was only pretending not to be scared, was trying to hold back the sea with a piece of cardboard. She knew that her own part in all of this was, as always, to be the voice of reason, to be the fact which must be hated. Rose knew that were she to take Adelle gently in her arms, talk about the scare, it would do no good. Adelle needed to yell, needed to try to scare the monster of fear away.

Yet, all Rose's knowledge, all her knowing, did no good. She felt her anger building, as it always did in such times. And even though Adelle was about to enter purgatory, she felt her own hatred rising. She hated the endless defenses, the blindness about Evan, the way Adelle used her to spare others. She even hated the folds and rolls in Adelle's body.

Still, always the philosopher, Rose analyzed her hatred. This was how her own mother had dealt with life. Denial and anger were good blotters for love or fear. They soaked it all up, didn't leave much of a stain, and allowed dryness the next day. Adelle's blotter was endless papers and plots and practices: envelopes, engagements, and avoidance. Rose sat on the sofa as Adelle packed up her papers for Mr. Wang.

She spoke to Evan, who had been sitting at the table reading the paper throughout the whole scene, pretending not to be a part of it, yet waiting to be called upon to act as hero.

Adelle stood above him, her voice controlled. "Evan?"

He looked up as though awakened from deep thought. "Huh?"

"Evan. Rose won't take me to the post office, and I have to get something off to a business associate before my surgery. Would you mind taking me?"

Evan, wiping crumbs off his chin, stood up slowly,

allowing the crumbs to fall from his lap onto the floor. "Whatever my lovely number one daughter wants. Let me just go upstairs and get some decent clothes on since we'll be going right on to the hospital. Honey," he said, climbing the stairs, "I think Rose is just a bit upset about this simple surgery thing. You and me, now we know it's nothing. We'll get you to the post office, get your stuff off, and get you to the hospital with time to spare. You can depend on your old dad." His voice trailed off as he entered his room.

Adelle gave Rose a dirty look and sat, stiffly, waiting for him to get back down.

Times such as these totally disabled Rose's ability to function in a rational manner. Her only solution was to resort to her Charlie Chaplin routine. She took the feather dust mop out of the broom closet, and began to brush the crumbs from where Evan had been sitting. She brushed the table, the chairs, the hanging lamp above the table. She was just getting ready for the coup de grace, that of brushing Adelle herself, when Evan popped down.

"Let's go, baby. Your man's ready."

As they sped off in the car, the dust flying in Rose's face, she waited until they were out of earshot, and then yelled, "Ha!"

* * * * *

Rose had parked her car and was walking towards the hospital when she saw Adelle walking in front of her. Evan must have let her out and gone to park the car. Rose walked as quickly as she could trying to catch up, but Adelle was in her business-woman's

139

walk, and therefore was moving like lightning. The faster Rose went, it seemed, the faster Adelle went. It was almost as if Adelle knew Rose was trying to catch up with her. "Bitch," Rose thought to herself, immediately feeling guilty for the thought, whereupon she almost bumped into Adelle who had stopped.

"Hi, Sweetie." It was as though nothing had happened. Typical Adelle.

"Hi yourself," Rose replied with resignation.

"I told Evan I'd wait for him, but he must be having a hard time parking. I'm going to have to admit myself. Will you wait and bring him along when he comes? You remember where the admitting desk is."

"Sure."

Adelle went in by herself, leaving Rose to wait for her favorite human in the universe. When he finally came along, he was looking cheerful, his baldness shining like a halo. "Where'd my baby go? Rose, you let that little girl go off by herself, her in the state she's in? I just can't trust nothing to you, can I?"

Inside, they found Adelle in a big chair reading the Bible, which had been the closest thing at hand. She didn't look up as Rose and Evan came in. Evan went right over to the desk, saying in his loudest voice, "I'm the daddy of that purdy little gal over there, here to see you folks treat my baby right." He smiled at the young receptionist.

"Well," she said, "I could see by the spring in your step that you weren't here for treatment for yourself."

He laughed happily. "I don't plan to leave her side till it's all over."

Just then a nurse came through the door.

"Adelle?" she called, and the big swinging door marked HOLDING swallowed Adelle up.

Rose planned to walk the hills of San Francisco, coming back now and then to check on Adelle. The thought of eight hours or more with Evan, especially when she was so worried, was just overwhelming.

"Evan. First they dope her up, then they operate, then they wait to make sure it all went well, wait for her to wake up again. Once she goes under, there's no need for me to be around. I'll take a short walk, come back for a check, and then, if all's well, I thought maybe I'd go look at the house I grew up in, school I went to. Things like that."

"Listen, darlin'. I plan to sit in that room with her till her little eyes close, then I'm out here like a soldier, waiting till she needs me again. Don't matter much if you're around or not. Could be you might even want to just go on back home, let a man take care of this."

"Thanks, Evan," Rose said wearily. "I'll be back in about an hour."

She walked a few blocks, but her heart wasn't in it. The day was sunny but cold. Rose knew that she was the one who should be at Adelle's bedside, that she should be the one holding Adelle's hand. Her own cowardice angered her. Still she knew that the situation between Evan and Adelle was so volatile, so unresolved that anyone stepping into it, even her, was an outsider asking for trouble. It was at that very moment, the very moment that Rose was thinking such thoughts, that she saw a person she had gone to high school with so long ago, in this city by the Bay. They passed each other, and he didn't recognize her. But for a moment, she was back there, back at Lowell, the smart skinny little girl with few friends, endless fears, and a home life as hard to bear as a wet wool blanket in a rainstorm. That, she guessed, was where Adelle was with Evan, always back in time, always trying to take a step or two into today. She got a cup of coffee and went back to the hospital. Evan was sitting in the waiting room, and jumped up, obviously glad to see her. He began talking almost as soon as he saw her.

"Rose. Well, she's under the knife now, but not to worry. I met 'em all, checked 'em all over. The surgeon is a nice old fellow, and the guy that put her to sleep, he's a good old-fashioned Catholic, just like me. And them two perky little nurses are just as sweet as can be." He winked. "I think one of 'em took a shine to me."

He paused, sat down, and patted the seat next to him, meaning for Rose to sit also. "I spent the waiting time right there in the room with poor Adelle, and they could all see how concerned I was. They all told me I looked fit as a fiddle. This operation stuff ain't near as bad as I thought."

They sat for a while, Evan acting like he was sitting in a chair crawling with ants. Finally he said, "You keep vigil for a while, will ya, while I go and take these weary bones for a walk down the hallway, see if I can find me a pretty nurse to pinch. Tain't good for an old man to be away from women too long." He winked and patted Rose on the knee, then whispered, "Hell, what am I saying? I ain't old. Sure ain't old enough to know better." He laughed, stood up, and stretched towards the ceiling, the rim of his Fruit of the Loom showing above his plaid walking shorts and below his polyester shirt. "Nope, tain't

142

good for a man to sit too long without bothering a female. They might forget we exist." He slapped Rose on the knee again, and left to wander the halls.

Rose picked up the Bible, and began to read about how the world began, who began it, and what it was like to live under rules chiseled in stone. It was, as she read it, not a lifestyle she would opt for. As she sat reading, people came and went, some checking in, some checking out, most just waiting for an outcome on someone they loved. She wondered how many of them believed in the Bible. Someone once said there are no atheists in foxholes. Might be true for hospitals too, though the only god Rose had ever worshipped was truth, perhaps the most elusive of deities.

When Evan got back, he smelled of beer. "Sorry I was gone so long. Got to feeling a bit dry, so I went to have a cool one. Course, with my luck, there was a little gal there needed cheering up. Lord, the sad tales some of these poor old gals got. Need someone to share it with, they do. Lucky for them, I'm always available with an ear and a beer."

"They came in just a while ago. Adelle did fine, and she's almost awake enough to make it home now. I'm just waiting. You can go on if you want."

Evan sat down like a ton of bricks. "I brung her in, and I'll bring her out."

Rose was wise enough not to argue with brick walls. "Well then, I'll get on home, get things ready. Drive carefully, Evan. Avoid the bumps if you can."

"I been drivin' since you was peeing in your diapers. Get yourself home."

Rose left. The traffic was bad, but the sunset was lovely. She picked up some flowers at a little street

stand. The Bible started with "In the beginning . . ."
She wondered what kind of a book it would have
been had it started, "At the end . . ." The pinks and
oranges of the sky billowed on the clouds, and as the
day cooled both its temperature and its lights, Rose
said to herself, "Thank you, God."

* * * * *

She had only been home a short while when Evan
and Adelle arrived. Adelle looked terrible: tired,
blotchy, and vague. Evan began talking at once.

"Well, here she is, her daddy's little girl. Looking
fit as a fiddle, ain't she? And this here little gal is in
tiptop shape. Ain't you, honey?" He squeezed Adelle.
"Now get your ass upstairs, and don't get out of that
bed till I tell you to, hear?"

Rose helped Adelle upstairs and into bed. Adelle
fell into the bed, and looked at Rose closely. Rose
could see that the scare was gone. She could also see
that Adelle was about to make a major statement.
Maybe she had had an out of body experience,
perhaps had found the meaning of life. Rose sat on
the cot, and reached for Adelle's hand. "What is it,
Adelle? I'm here." She was fully attentive.

Adelle clutched her right breast, her heart line left
behind in the operating room, and leaned forward.
She whispered, though it was obvious that she was
capable of normal speech: "Never," she whispered,
with an emphasis few could give to a whisper, "*never*
go to a holding room with Evan."

Rose had thought the sky might shake with what
Adelle's first words were after facing possible death.
She thought the walls of the bedroom might drip

144

blood or spit forth diamonds. But Adelle was going to talk about, of all things, Evan. Rose remembered that she had learned in therapy that we all create our own reality, that we reap what we sow, that nothing happens to us without our allowing it to. She humbled herself, ready to accept her fate.

"Evan —" And here Adelle looked at Rose as though she had solved the riddle of the universe, "— actually came into the holding room after you left, and he *made passes* at all the females. Rose, he even called an M.D. 'nursie.' He invited them all out to lunch, to come visit him in Bakersfield. He talked to a man going in for major surgery, telling the man all about his own small ailments, his own good health. He was gross, Rose, and a total embarrassment. The topper was, the worst of all, he asked *Janice* for a 'hot date.' The very doctor who was so kind to me last time. Why didn't you come in with me, Rose?"

Rose noticed for the first time that the poster behind Adelle's bed was hung lopsided. It was a poster of a baby owl, looking out at the world with big eyes.

Adelle shook her head. "Maybe he's senile."

Just then Evan came upstairs, beer in hand, and acted as if Rose were a bedpost. He talked only to Adelle. "What does my little girl want? Anything? Hell's bells. I remember the last time you was in the hospital. Was for your little tonsils. I remember that as if it were yesterday. You were so sick, and I sat by your bed. It was about five in the morning and your little throat hurt, so I went out to get you some ice cream. Seems like yesterday." He drained his beer and handed the empty can to Rose. "Get me another one, will you, Rose?"

145

Rose walked downstairs slowly, pretending she heard Adelle rise up from her pillow, and shout, with the years of rage she always kept clutched in her heart, "Get out of here!" But no such luck. She took her time in the kitchen, deciding to put her spices in alphabetical order. By the time she was up to the C's, the cumin and coriander and cinnamon, she was bored, so she took Evan up his beer.

As she re-entered the room, she thought of herself as a warrior from *Dune*. She showed no emotion. She saw the life-giving drops of water hanging in a cave which only the pure might enter. Evan grabbed his beer in slow-motion as the frames slowed to a snail's pace. He slowly reached out to touch Rose. His old face and his old hand and his old thoughts were like mud on the sunlight silent on the floor of the bedroom. She took her magic sword and cut the chain which bound the sleeping princess to the aged evil keeper of the secret. The maiden leapt from the bed, still in slow-motion, and moved to kiss Rose, to reward her for her bravery.

The spell was broken as Adelle spoke, softly. "Evan, could you possibly hand me a glass of water?"

Evan wiped his nose clean with his cloth handkerchief, and Rose hoped he kept his soul cleaner than he did his handkerchief. He poured some water out of the chilled container Rose had put by the bed. "Thank you, Evan," Adelle managed, and then fell asleep. Evan lay down on the cot which was Rose's bed of late and closed his eyes.

Rose went downstairs to cook up something for dinner. She had made some soup the day before thinking that Adelle might be too sick to eat, but Evan would probably want something more robust.

She decided on meatloaf and mashed potatoes. As she worked, she thought of her own father. Wise, no. Intelligent, yes. His brains were much bigger than his penis, but the latter ruled the former. He took no responsibility for that though. His loves, lordy, his wounded children and his dying wife were strewn over the landscape. The man could easily order the correct wine in any of twenty languages, but he couldn't say good night and make anyone feel safe. So many families were nothing but broken heaps of seaweed, drifting in and out of lonely coves, never realizing that they had been cut off, permanently, from the safety of the sands.

Still, having been dismissed by Evan, Rose stood tall in her kitchen. Rose, who could march across the earth, who could make with loving hands the richest of breads, who could grow grain and grin as she did, tried to be caring enough to let Adelle seek her own peace in her own way, even if it meant the flotsam and jetsam of Evan. Rose decided it was okay to cart beers and think her thoughts.

Later Evan came down, and turned on the TV. He seemed lost when he didn't have something to boom about, some woman to harass or hassle. She never had liked him, but she never really hated him. Actually, at times she pitied him. The poor old man, having messed up his wives and his kid, was now into pretending to be the Rambo of the operating room.

Later when she went upstairs to check on Adelle, she noticed that the poster was straight. There were *some* nice things about Evan. She bent to kiss Adelle on the forehead, and Adelle muttered from somewhere in her sleep, "The question is, how many points can

147

we get?" And Rose knew, knew for a fact, that she would pull through.

* * * * *

The next morning Rose was drinking her coffee, eating her Danish, and Evan came down, all shaved and smelling of Old Spice. He had on long pants instead of shorts, and shoes and socks instead of slippers. He rubbed his hands together. "Well, looks like a fine day to hit the road. Figure I've done my thing. They say fish and house guests start smelling poorly after a while. Been a pleasure. I'll just wait till my gal gets up, then I'll be off."

Rose heard the slowly swelling sound of a symphony somewhere in the hills. She felt long flowing robes of soft golden threads appear upon her body. She danced lovingly, high on ballerina toes, to get Evan his cup of coffee. As he sat down, she hovered above the table lifted by the beauty of the music. Then she sat down across from him. "You sure, Evan?"

"I seen my duty, and I done it." He laughed. So, for once, did Rose.

"Let me pack you something to eat, something for the trip."

"You're a good little gal, Rose. I don't hardly ever tell you that. You cook funny food, but it tastes good. Don't bother with nothing. I can stop on the road."

In spite of what Evan said, Rose began to make some sandwiches, as he began to read the sports section to her.

"Listen to this here. You read this? This coach,

148

I'm sure you never heard of him, but he's got a brain tumor. Now wouldn't that be a bitch? Imagine there he is, top of his field, and he's got this crappy cancer thing. Shit, I wonder what that would be like?"

A bit later Adelle came down, looking sleepy, her breast clutched lightly. She looked out at the pond and spoke to Evan. "Well, I guess you're on your way. I see Rose got you your breakfast. All packed?"

Evan looked at the pond at about the same point Adelle seemed to be watching. "Reckon. Yes, I reckon I am. And I reckon a father what's got a lovely daughter like you deserves a big daughter-like kiss. Come on, lay one on me."

Adelle turned to kiss Evan on the cheek, and he grabbed her, holding her tightly. She let out a cry of pain, then said firmly, "You're holding me too tight, Evan. It hurts."

He dropped his arms as one might drop a log with a large spider on it.

"Sorry."

He seemed embarrassed and lost. He seemed out of place. The bond between them was breaking again, as it did each time he left. It was his desertion all over again.

Adelle touched his arm. "It's okay, Evan. It's just that I've had this major surgery and it hurts if you touch me too hard. Even if you mean it nicely."

Adelle could over explain in such a way that anyone's guilt or discomfort immediately ballooned beyond endurance. Evan grabbed up his bags, and took them out to his car.

He came back in, pulled out his wallet, and handed Adelle a one hundred dollar bill. "This here is

149

for any phone calls I might have made. If that don't cover it, just let me know. Anything left over, that's yours to keep."

He looked at Rose, smiling. "You know, you should have been the owner of a restaurant or the mother of ten kids. Hell, I never seen a woman so much into mothering." He handed Rose a fifty dollar bill. "This here's to take a break from that damned kitchen of yours and take my gal out to dinner. Some place fancy, now, and remind 'em that the tab's on me."

As Evan turned his car around, Rose and Adelle stood in the driveway, each of them clutching her monetary reward. Evan rolled down the window and headed off, yelling as he did: "Call ya in a week."

Rose and Adelle looked at each other for a moment. Then Adelle smiled an evil smile and said, waving her bill, "Mine's bigger than yours is." And just to prove a point, though she wasn't sure what it was, Rose tossed her bill into the air, and the wind carried it over the hills, and down the side of the gulf. "So what," she said, and she smiled.

* * * * *

They stood in the bathroom, the wall-sized mirror in front of them. Adelle was naked except for her bandages. They looked at each other through the mirror, not face to face.

"Ready?"

Rose nodded. They began, slowly, to pull off the tape. It went way around the back, and covered

150

almost half of the front. What would be left? The bandages were so tight that it was impossible to know.

Rose peeled away a part, and fluids poured down Adelle's back. The heat and adhesive had caused large water blisters which burst as the tape was pulled off. Rose thought that she might vomit. She removed more and more adhesive until it was barely clinging to the front of Adelle's body. Rose felt quite faint. Adelle was being her stoical self, watching her new body about to emerge without saying a word.

Surgeons did not tell one what was left, only that the cancer was, they hoped, gone. What did a bit of breast, fatty tissue to boot, mean to a man with a knife? If you went to a butcher to buy meat, you were told pound-wise and ounce-wise what you had bought. When some of you was removed and tossed into the hazardous waste container, you didn't get told anything.

Rose went to lie down in the bedroom. "I have to take a break, Adelle. I'm feeling a little woozy." She had only been on the cot a moment when Adelle called. "Rose. Come on in. It's done. Come look. Tell me what you think."

Rose went back and together she and Adelle looked in the mirror. It was too soon to look at Adelle straight on. The scar was long, not savage looking, and the breast seemed to be mostly there.

"I think I match more or less. Is that a correct interpretation of the facts? I really would prefer to match."

Adelle did seem to match. The smallness of the

right as compared to the left was not all that noticeable. "Well," Adelle said, "I guess I won't need to spend hundreds of dollars for a prosthesis."

They looked away from the mirror and into each other's eyes. There were tears in Adelle's eyes as she said again, "I guess I'm okay, Rose. I match."

* * * * *

Day broke, and Rose awoke feeling light and airy. Evan would not walk down the stairs, smile his toothless smile, and then pee on the bathroom floor. Rose would have the morning to herself again. Downstairs, she put on her glasses to walk to the mailbox, and noticed a song building in her heart.

Now Rose's mother had not been much of a gift giver, but usually after she screamed how much she hated Rose, when her guilt was heavy and the air was thick, she would say, "Rose, you have bounce. No matter what I do to you, you can bounce back." Rose had always thought that an odd sentence for a mother to make, but she heard it so often she believed it. It was one of the reasons why, in moments of despair or truly heavy rains, Rose often found her vocal cords, and burst into fits of uncontrollable singing. Now, Gulliver by her side, she sang a short medley of Perry Como hits, just the happy ones. Then, there it was, the newspaper, in the same old puddle of dried mud. It was going to be a good day.

She wished, and had always wished, that she knew how to tap dance. Or maybe play spoons. It was all the same, the many faces of happiness. What can you say to a big wake-up sky, a dog who lumbers along beside you, a person who cares, and enough sunlight to play with every shadow on earth? Rose reached over and touched Gulliver. His head was as high as her chest. "Shit, Gully, Great day, no?" Gulliver, not breaking stride, brushed his body against hers. He knew.

Rose hugged Gulliver goodbye, put the paper inside, got the car keys, and off she went for the morning's sweet rolls. She decided to get some rock salt and cream for homemade ice cream, some fresh squeezed (right before your eyes) grapefruit juice, and some Mexican cactus leaves, just because she had never cooked them before. Tonight would be homemade tamales, cactus leaf salad, and lemon ice cream.

She drove home the back way, up the work-a-day streets, just as the traffic was beginning to pick up, the sun slanting meanly over the blacktop. She still had a song in her heart. Years ago, when she and Adelle were in therapy, it was a given that what happened to a person was caused by that person. The therapists had once said, "We refuse to accept that World War Two ever occurred. It may have taken place in your life, but not in ours." They always spoke as one, and totally negated any pain on the face of the planet. "Hitler did not live in our lifetime."

Rose, thinking back, thought that maybe there was less terror in her life than she had supposed. She and Adelle had met cancer, and so far it seemed like something which could be handled. It was something, perhaps, which love could get you through.

So, as the sun screamed at the earth to come to life, as that great ball of fire pleaded with others to join in the dance, Rose knew that she loved Adelle. It was one of those days. When given a bit of morning solitude, Rose was a dynamo of love. She stopped by the VCR store and checked out *The Music Man*. It was the kind of day for a romance. On the way home she hummed "Goodnight My Someone."

* * * * *

Rose and Adelle had eaten dinner, had watched the movie, and it was nice. It was nice to watch two people fall in love on the screen, watch them fight the feeling, then melt, go with it, and walk off into the sunset, arms around each other, music swelling against the credits.

They walked upstairs, partly themselves, partly the film lovers they had just spent time with. Rose was still using the cot, though they often held hands for awhile before they slept.

"I'm so glad it's over, Rose, glad it's done with."

"You were very brave. Through it all, you were *very* brave."

"I was scared."

"I know."

"It takes a lot of courage to go on, to fight. The pain is what makes it all so hard. Even with the right attitude, the pain can pull you down."

Rose was quiet. She had never felt physical pain, didn't know its power.

"Some mornings it's like a shower of knives and razor blades. Some mornings I don't think I can make it. But I do. I do, don't I?"

"Yes."

"It helped me to have Evan around. I didn't really have him here for you."

"I know."

"I don't know why. Sometimes I don't think I even like him. I certainly don't like being his number one daughter."

"Ah, Adelle. Things only have the meanings we give them. What matters is that you, for some reason, a reason which makes sense in some true part of you, need to have Evan in your life. And he, for his reasons, needs to have you."

"What would you have done if I had died, Rose?"

At that moment, moonlight swept into the room, lighting up Adelle's face with a soft warmth. Rose didn't answer the question, and they fell asleep holding hands.

* * * * *

Once, years ago, when Rose and Adelle had spent a few weeks at a fall-apart cabin on a desolate beach near Mexico, Rose had learned something about Adelle which she still didn't understand. Rose, having read a book on sexual fantasies of women, asked Adelle to share one. Adelle, wearing number fifteen sun protector, and a hat which covered her face as well as her head, and a towel draped over her body in case the sun protector didn't work, told her fantasy.

"Well," she began, "I worked on this one a long time."

Rose wondered how one could work on a sexual fantasy, or why one would.

"I am in a huge beehive, but it is made out of a

smooth black velvet-like material. There are all these women who are sort of half bee, half woman. It is their job to feed me, and they do this by filling their mouths with something sort of like yogurt, and then putting it into my vagina. Then they sort of buzz around while I turn it into honey, and they have to lick it out. If it isn't done right, of course, they face death."

Rose, to keep from laughing, kicked a bit of sand with her toe and watched some pelicans swim over the sea in formation. "You hate yogurt."

"Rose. You weren't listening. I don't have anything to do with the yogurt. The bee ladies do."

"What flavor yogurt would you suppose it is?"

Very mysteriously, Adelle replied. "Who knows?"

That night Rose was a bee lady, Adelle was the queen, and the flavor was peach, Rose's favorite.

Now, years later, sex itself had become a fantasy. Rose missed making love, missed the old fire that had warmed so many a night. The books, the doctors, all had said that it took time to get back to making love. Partly it was psychological, and partly it was the hormones which were a part of the treatment.

It was not something they could talk about. They hadn't talked about sex even when it was a rich and present part of their lives. Rose could wait, but it was hard. Sometimes love was like one of the fabled black holes of outer space, something so huge, so bright, that its own power kept anything from leaving, anything from entering. It was a prisoner of its own energy.

Time drifted by, and Rose and Adelle drifted apart. They hadn't really spoken in weeks. They'd

156

talked, but only about things. They'd talk about things which were outside them, but not about themselves, not about love. They'd reached out, held hands, beds apart, at night, but it felt lonely. There was no play, no silliness, none of the fun which was the life-blood of their relationship. The relationship had become like two cows staring at each other across some cow-plopped field. Rose wished for something from the past, anything but the seriousness which had fallen with a thud on their lives. She wished Adelle would steal something from the refrigerator, not understand a headline, talk to a wall by mistake.

But they didn't make mistakes any more. They made progress. Life was moving at a different pace, one out of keeping with their love. It was like trying to breathe as the rapids were carrying you along. It was all gulp and sink, with the sunned sky flashing gold for moments as ones eyes were swallowed by the churning waters and the lungs begged for peace.

* * * * *

A full month, to the day, after the lymph nodes surgery, Adelle was, at last, well enough, healed enough, to take a bath instead of a shower. She hadn't told Rose what she was planning. It was her big surprise. Rose was downstairs, back from her trip to the bakery, when Adelle's voice urged her upstairs. "Rose, hurry. Come on up. I want to show you something."

There was a blood-rushing-through-your-veins urgency, and Rose flew. There sat Adelle, her face mottled from the heat, steam pouring from the

157

waters, a smile more happy than Rose Penski had seen in a long time. "Look, Rose. I can take a bath again."

Adelle looked so tiny in the tub although she was a normal-size woman. To Rose she seemed like some Norman Rockwell painting of a toddler sitting in an old-fashioned wash tub, a mama wiping her hands on an apron worn round the waist.

"My God," said Rose, smiling back. "Just plain old my God."

"Hurts like hell."

"Maybe the water's too hot. Usually boiling water is a bit uncomfortable for the human body."

Adelle splashed some water at her. It was like the good old days.

Rose sat on the counter next to the sink. "Adelle, this is wondrous. You can be totally clean now. You can wipe the filth and grime from your pussy, as Evan might say. You can wash all the odors of life down the drain. You can join the land of the clean. Who knows what's next? Maybe you'll be able to hook your own bra."

"Hand me a towel, would you, Sweetie? Then heat me up an apple fritter. I believe I could eat an army."

Rose Penski laughed, threw her happiness up to the bathroom skylight in great thunders of happiness. "Adelle, my dear, you mean you could eat *like* an army. Very few civilized people would want to eat *an* army. That is, unless you really have expanded your food yearnings."

"Whatever," said Adelle, letting Rose dry her back

as she stood, wringing the water from her long blonde hair. "Any kind of food will do."

As Adelle dressed, Rose went to prepare an instant feast. She called out the window to Gulliver. "Hey, Gully old boy, a new journey is about to begin." He wagged his tail.

As is usual with life, the first miracle brought with it an avalanche of miracles. In a few days, Adelle was, indeed, hooking her own bra. It took close to a minute, and pain hung from her face, but she managed. Though Rose was used to seeing Adelle use her body the way most drivers use fifth gear, it was amazing. She could only wonder at the energy such a once simple act took.

She applauded, laughing. "Adelle, the *Guiness Book of Records* if anything ever was."

Adelle smiled. "I am pretty amazing, aren't I?"

Then it came, the big moment of truth. It was another soft summer night, and Rose lay on her cot, thinking about life, wondering if animals felt the emotion *anger.* Adelle's voice sounded as though it were coming from another planet, so taken aback was Rose.

"I'd like to see if we can make love."

Now Rose Penski had faced many challenges when making love. One woman had only liked to make love on stairways, which required great balancing skills, and superhuman strength. Rose had made love in the ocean at Coney Island, losing the bottom of her bathing suit in the process. She had to leave the beach wrapped in a white terrycloth towel with HILTON in raised white letters, very much aware that Hilton did not serve its guests human-size towels. She had even made love on the top floor of the Empire State Building, all personnel having gone home except a night watchperson who tapped on the office door every thirty minutes.

But never had Rose made love to see if someone could. It was a bit like *Tea and Sympathy*. Adelle wanted to prove herself, her prowess. Actually, Rose thought, she wanted to check out her full arm movement.

Rose, who had been living a rather active fantasy life of late, much of it having to do simply with Adelle's recovery, found that she was drifting from the scene. She wished she were in a blue lagoon near Marlon Brando's Tahitian Isle. She wished she were climbing a set of glimmering silver stairs, her high-heeled feet tapping out accompaniment to some trumpet solo. She wished, as Adelle leaned over and kissed the tip of her nose, that she were playing a piano on some moonlit deck, fingers moving with sensual swiftness, red nails making a slight click as they tickled the ivories.

Rose climbed carefully onto the bed. Adelle wrapped her arms around her, and uttered one word. "Aggggg." It was a word of pain. She moved her hand to her breast and spread her mouth lengthwise into a smiling grimace. "We'll have to wait a second until the pain goes away." She cried out again.

"I guess, Rose," she said in a moment, "that the time is not yet ripe."

"I guess, Adelle, that it will take a while."

"I love you."

"And I love you."

They hugged a careful painless hug, and Adelle

turned so that her wounded body was comfortable. Rose fell asleep almost at once and dreamed that she was the person who discovered King Tut's tomb. Inside the sacred pyramid, the moon shafts slid down a secret tunnel, leading Rose to the young king's casket, its golden cover holding the moonlight in metallic puddles of shine. Rose, in the dream, found the meaning of life. When she awoke the next morning, she held the feeling, not the message. Again, it had escaped her.

* * * * *

The next evening they watched *Passage to India* on the VCR, and Adelle went upstairs to do her exercises. Half an hour each morning, half an hour each night, Adelle had to walk her fingers up the wall, stretch her arms towards heaven as if picking apples from a tree.

Rose lay on the bed, very tired for some reason, ready to drop off. "I'm up to ten minutes without a break now, Rose, ten minutes before the pain is unbearable. I'm used to the steady unceasing pain, but the deep knife-cutting pain I can only endure for ten minutes. How's that for progress?" she asked happily.

"I'm proud of you, Adelle. You haven't missed a day of doing your exercises." Rose yawned. "I'm going to just shut my eyes for a minute here. I'll wake up when you crawl into bed."

Adelle, not breaking pace, grunted yes, and continued her workout.

Rose awakened several life spans later to discover Adelle tying her foot to the wooden bedpost with the piece of clothesline she had been using to do her stretching exercises. It had been a joke with them for all the years, that Rose wanted Adelle to tie her to a bedpost in a sexual frenzy.

Years ago, Rose had worked with a German woman whose boyfriend used to tie her to the bedpost, and she had made it sound simply wonderful. Once, too, Rose had had a short affair with a woman who was into S & M. They would read pornography each night before they went to sleep. Rose had read more about crazed Turks and Latin sex fiends than was good for any human. Thus, her desire to be tied to a bedpost. She had not, however, planned to be tied to a bed by a pain-driven cancer patient who was using a rope worn thin by breast exercises.

Having read all of Houdini's books, Rose wiggled her toes once and was as free as a bird. Adelle looked astounded.

"How did you do that? I thought I had that tighter than the lid on a childproof aspirin bottle."

"Secret of the trade."

"Rose. We have to make love, we just have to. I'm not sure I even remember how."

"It's like riding a bike. You never forget."

"Rose. When can we make love? What if I never regain my strength? What if I never win back the full use of my arms?"

"I got it," Rose said, never one to let a problem lie about unsolved, "let's set a date, a goal. How about our ninth anniversary? I believe we have that one coming up in a few days."

Adelle smiled. "I thought you had forgotten. You didn't mention it."

"My birthday and our anniversary are two dates I never forget. On each I began living."

"Aw shucks," said Adelle, hiding the fact that she was touched.

"We can plan a magnificent banquet, a few long-winded speeches from the major participants, and then a night of passion. Think you can work that into your schedule?"

"I believe I can alter my schedule, that is, for a magnificent banquet, and a night of passion."

"Don't forget the long-winded speeches."

"That's your domain. My speech will be short, swift, and to the point, but heartfelt."

"And Adelle, no offense, but we can leave the rope out of it?"

"I thought you liked that sort of stuff."

"I did, in my youth. But as a budding matron, I believe it ill suits me. Now perhaps I might like to have my body strewn with flower petals, then have them blown off by the soft warm breath of a lover, one petal at a time."

"Oh Rose. That sounds wonderful."

Rose had amazed even herself. "It does, doesn't it?" she said in wonderment.

* * * * *

July 27th, and it was the anniversary, number nine. Nine years of sharing life. Rose awoke to a blue sky, the clear high kind of sky which only comes in the western states. She planned to make Moo Shi Roo Pork for dinner. It was Adelle's all time favorite. They would watch *South Pacific* on the VCR, which was sort of their song package. When they had first become involved, Rose suggested that she and Adelle have a song, a song which would remind them of their love each time they heard it.

"We can't have a song," Adelle had pouted, "because all the really good songs have been taken by your past loves. There's not a good free song left." So they had more or less chosen the whole of *South Pacific* as their song, although neither of them wanted to be Mitzi Gaynor.

Adelle went off to the office, and Rose took the day to prepare for the night. Dollars sat watching her as she began to cook.

"It will go well, Dollars. It will. We will have a lovely evening, and Adelle will be able to make love. It's gonna work because it's gotta work because I say so."

Dollars wagged her tail, which Rose took for encouragement.

"Thanks buddy." She went over and gave the dog a pat.

* * * * *

Rose and Adelle sat down to watch *South Pacific* on the VCR. The Mandarin pancakes were steaming, the richly spiced pork shreds lying next to artfully carved spring onions. The plum sauce looked rich and dark. Rose had also peeled some orange segments, mixed them with barely cooked asparagus spears, and sprinkled them with a light sauce of sugar, sake, and rice vinegar.

Adelle wore a white floor-length gown with a slender sash of green and blue. Rose, who had spent

164

most of the day in the kitchen and was quite hot, wore only her grey Ocean Pacific shorts which were spotted from her kitchen work. It was, she figured, too hot for tops. Her breasts, which were once the size of kiwi fruits, now bounced as she walked. They were the kind which would not respond well to a lumpectomy: too pendulous.

Adelle, looking cool and elegant, balanced her food-laden plate on her knee and said to Rose, "I find your dress code less than adequate."

Rose, tired besides being hot, was in a good mood. She went into Evan's bathroom, pulled off a good two feet of toilet paper and fashioned herself a tie with a smart knot.

"Okay now?" she asked.

"I want one too," said Adelle.

So after a few moments' work, they watched *South Pacific* in identical toilet tissue ties, flipping them up in Oliver Hardy style as the plot demanded.

They each opened the fortune cookies Rose had bought to go with the meal. They both got the same fortune: "A swan in the moonlight has no shadow." It made no sense to them, but they laughed that both were the same.

As Nellie Forbush and Emile De Becque joined hands against the backdrop of the Pacific Ocean, Rose brought out the small heart-shaped cherry pie she had made, criss-crossing the dough so that it spelled out I LOVE YOU.

They took it, some plates, and two after-dinner cordials of Drambuie upstairs. They were prepared to give it one more try. Adelle slipped out of her gown, and Rose slipped out of her shorts. There was a mere sliver of light from the new moon, and it was visible only in a small corner of the window. A cool breeze, gentle as down, played against Rose's naked skin, causing ripples of icy tingles to pass down her spine.

They sat on the bed, eating the pie without utensils, picking off bits of the crusty I LOVE YOU, dipping them in the sweet red juices, licking fingers, touching lips. It surprised them both at how easy it was to make love, after all the failed attempts of late. Almost before either knew what was happening, they were eating each other as they had eaten the pie, finding warm wet places with their lips, tongues.

They lay for awhile, amazed at the passion which had found them, amazed that they had let it. Rose picked her glass of Drambuie off the night table, and handed Adelle hers. They toasted each other, and Adelle, sounding throaty and sensual, spoke Rose's name, softly, as if to ask a question. "Rose?"

Rose took a sip of her drink, felt the smooth warmth fall down her throat. "Yes, my dear Adelle. What is it?"

"I just don't see how a swan in the moonlight can have no shadow. Explain it to me."

Rose, knowing that it made no sense, said, anyway, "Don't you see, Adelle. It was a black swan."

"Oh," said Adelle with seriousness, "now I get it."

Inwardly Rose said, "Say goodnight, Gracie," but outwardly she said, simply, "Happy anniversary. I love you."

"I love you too, Sweetie."

* * * * *

166

A few days after their anniversary dinner, Adelle began her radiation treatment, which was to last for five weeks. Rose would go with her to the university hospital, a different one from where she had been operated on, and sit in the waiting room as Adelle was zapped with invisible rays. She had been tattooed with a few little black dots on her chest so the x-ray technicians would know just where to place the large machine. They would then leave the room, and turn it on for the allotted amount of time.

Adelle would come away drained. Her skin looked red and burned, and it was hard, sometimes impossible, for her to eat. Rose made rice pudding, fruit salads, loaves of oatmeal bread. Sometimes Adelle could eat, sometimes not. Often after a treatment she'd stay in bed for a day, maybe even two.

So it was that the month of August passed. Then, sweet heaven, it was over. The mighty medical profession had done all it could to spare her life. Adelle had done her part as well. She had faced her illness, and made the choices which were right for her.

"I might not live another month, Rose. You know that, don't you?"

"And you might outlive me."

"That's doubtful."

"Let's do something wild, Adelle, something wild and out of character."

Adelle looked excited. "What?"

"Let's join a support group, see what's going on with other human beings."

"You mean cancer patients?"

"Well, more like breast cancer. It might do us good to be around others such as we."

"Heavens, Rose. There's no one like us."

"If you say yes, I promise to make a chocolate cheesecake with Bailey's Irish Cream."

"I don't know, Rose. The idea sounds scary."

"Okay. Pepper prawns. Veal scaloppine. Fried oysters. Name it."

"How about all of that, plus bouillabaisse tomorrow, and Rose's beignets for breakfast each Sunday for a month?"

"You drive a hard bargain, Adelle. I can see why you are such a big wheel in the realty game. But, I'm no match for you. You got it."

"Swear it?"

"Swear it."

"Well, now that you've promised, I have something to tell you, you old Rose Penski you. I went and signed us up for one this afternoon. Ha. Tricked you."

So they ate great food for the entire month of September, and began attending the support group. It was an all-woman group, so no husbands were there, but the women accepted Rose after a short period of feeling uncomfortable with the alternate lifestyle she and Adelle led.

They both got more into life. Adelle took up bird watching, and Rose began to read the *Wall Street Journal*.

They stayed in Fairfax through Christmas, celebrating with each other and the members of the support group. Sometimes at night Adelle trembled, covered with fear, and Rose would hold her, singing songs from old radio shows, or showing off her new business prowess by discussing the Dow Jones Average. They tried to go on at least one picnic a month.

* * * * *

They celebrated their twelfth anniversary on Sanibel Island, down near the Everglades of Florida. Adelle had finally lost a breast to cancer. It had happened a little more than a year after her first cancer diagnosis; it had been the other breast, her left one.

Now here they were, in the middle of winter, the sun a balmy seventy-five, the azure sea shining before them. They were standing on the little bridge between Sanibel and Captiva. Adelle was glued to something she had focused in the frame of her two-hundred dollar binoculars. "Rose. There is the most unusual bird out there. It hasn't moved since I brought it into view, and it has the most bizarre shape I've ever seen. Here, you take a look. Help me find it in the book."

Adelle tried to slip the binoculars off her neck, but they became tangled in the chain holding her glasses, and for a moment she appeared to be strangling herself. Finally, slightly out of breath, she passed the binoculars to Rose. Rose looked out to sea. She handed the glasses back to Adelle. "Adelle, that's a buoy, not a bird. Take another look."

Adelle did. "So it is. You're right. How silly of me." Her hat flopped in the wind, and small bits of her golden locks emerged from beneath the brim.

Rose Penski put her arm around Adelle's waist,

thinking as they walked back to the car that Adelle may have lost a breast, but she would never lose her charm.

A few of the publications of
THE NAIAD PRESS, INC.
P.O. Box 10543 • Tallahassee, Florida 32302
Phone (904) 539-5965
Mail orders welcome. Please include 15% postage.

THE BEVERLY MALIBU by Katherine V. Forrest. 288 pp. A
Kate Delafield Mystery. 3rd in a series. ISBN 0-941483-47-9 $16.95

THERE'S SOMETHING I'VE BEEN MEANING TO TELL
YOU Ed. by Loralee MacPike. 288 pp. Gay men and lesbians
coming out to their children. ISBN 0-941483-44-4   9.95
ISBN 0-941483-54-1   16.95

LIFTING BELLY by Gertrude Stein. Ed. by Rebecca Mark. 104
pp. Erotic poetry. ISBN 0-941483-51-7   8.95
ISBN 0-941483-53-3   14.95

ROSE PENSKI by Roz Perry. 192 pp. Adult lovers in a long-term
relationship. ISBN 0-941483-37-1   8.95

AFTER THE FIRE by Jane Rule. 256 pp. Warm, human novel
by this incomparable author. ISBN 0-941483-45-2   8.95

SUE SLATE, PRIVATE EYE by Lee Lynch. 176 pp. The gay
folk of Peacock Alley are *all* cats. ISBN 0-941483-52-5   8.95

CHRIS by Randy Salem. 224 pp. Golden oldie. Handsome Chris
and her adventures. ISBN 0-941483-42-8   8.95

THREE WOMEN by March Hastings. 232 pp. Golden oldie. A
triangle among wealthy sophisticates. ISBN 0-941483-43-6   8.95

RICE AND BEANS by Valeria Taylor. 232 pp. Love and
romance on poverty row. ISBN 0-941483-41-X   8.95

PLEASURES by Robbi Sommers. 204 pp. Unprecedented
eroticism. ISBN 0-941483-49-5   8.95

EDGEWISE by Camarin Grae. 372 pp. Spellbinding
adventure. ISBN 0-941483-19-3   9.95

FATAL REUNION by Claire McNab. 216 pp. 2nd Det. Inspec.
Carol Ashton mystery. ISBN 0-941483-40-1   8.95

KEEP TO ME STRANGER by Sarah Aldridge. 372 pp. Romance
set in a department store dynasty. ISBN 0-941483-38-X   9.95

HEARTSCAPE by Sue Gambill. 204 pp. American lesbian in
Portugal. ISBN 0-941483-33-9   8.95

IN THE BLOOD by Lauren Wright Douglas. 252 pp. Lesbian
science fiction adventure fantasy ISBN 0-941483-22-3   8.95

THE BEE'S KISS by Shirley Verel. 216 pp. Delicate, delicious
romance. ISBN 0-941483-36-3   8.95

RAGING MOTHER MOUNTAIN by Pat Emmerson. 264 pp.
Furosa Firechild's adventures in Wonderland. ISBN 0-941483-35-5   8.95

IN EVERY PORT by Karin Kallmaker. 228 pp. Jessica's sexy, adventuresome travels. ISBN 0-941483-37-7   8.95

OF LOVE AND GLORY by Evelyn Kennedy. 192 pp. Exciting WWII romance. ISBN 0-941483-32-0   8.95

CLICKING STONES by Nancy Tyler Glenn. 288 pp. Love transcending time. ISBN 0-941483-31-2   8.95

SURVIVING SISTERS by Gail Pass. 252 pp. Powerful love story. ISBN 0-941483-16-9   8.95

SOUTH OF THE LINE by Catherine Ennis. 216 pp. Civil War adventure. ISBN 0-941483-29-0   8.95

WOMAN PLUS WOMAN by Dolores Klaich. 300 pp. Supurb Lesbian overview. ISBN 0-941483-28-2   9.95

SLOW DANCING AT MISS POLLY'S by Sheila Ortiz Taylor. 96 pp. Lesbian Poetry ISBN 0-941483-30-4   7.95

DOUBLE DAUGHTER by Vicki P. McConnell. 216 pp. A Nyla Wade Mystery, third in the series. ISBN 0-941483-26-6   8.95

HEAVY GILT by Delores Klaich. 192 pp. Lesbian detective/ disappearing homophobes/upper class gay society.
ISBN 0-941483-25-8   8.95

THE FINER GRAIN by Denise Ohio. 216 pp. Brilliant young college lesbian novel. ISBN 0-941483-11-8   8.95

THE AMAZON TRAIL by Lee Lynch. 216 pp. Life, travel & lore of famous lesbian author. ISBN 0-941483-27-4   8.95

HIGH CONTRAST by Jessie Lattimore. 264 pp. Women of the Crystal Palace. ISBN 0-941483-17-7   8.95

OCTOBER OBSESSION by Meredith More. Josie's rich, secret Lesbian life. ISBN 0-941483-18-5   8.95

LESBIAN CROSSROADS by Ruth Baetz. 276 pp. Contemporary Lesbian lives. ISBN 0-941483-21-5   9.95

BEFORE STONEWALL: THE MAKING OF A GAY AND LESBIAN COMMUNITY by Andrea Weiss & Greta Schiller. 96 pp., 25 illus. ISBN 0-941483-20-7   7.95

WE WALK THE BACK OF THE TIGER by Patricia A. Murphy. 192 pp. Romantic Lesbian novel/beginning women's movement.
ISBN 0-941483-13-4   8.95

SUNDAY'S CHILD by Joyce Bright. 216 pp. Lesbian athletics, at last the novel about sports. ISBN 0-941483-12-6   8.95

OSTEN'S BAY by Zenobia N. Vole. 204 pp. Sizzling adventure romance set on Bonaire. ISBN 0-941483-15-0   8.95

LESSONS IN MURDER by Claire McNab. 216 pp. 1st Det. Inspec. Carol Ashton mystery — erotic tension!. ISBN 0-941483-14-2   8.95

YELLOWTHROAT by Penny Hayes. 240 pp. Margarita, bandit, kidnaps Julia. ISBN 0-941483-10-X 8.95

SAPPHISTRY: THE BOOK OF LESBIAN SEXUALITY by Pat Califia. 3d edition, revised. 208 pp. ISBN 0-941483-24-X 8.95

CHERISHED LOVE by Evelyn Kennedy. 192 pp. Erotic Lesbian love story. ISBN 0-941483-08-8 8.95

LAST SEPTEMBER by Helen R. Hull. 208 pp. Six stories & a glorious novella. ISBN 0-941483-09-6 8.95

THE SECRET IN THE BIRD by Camarin Grae. 312 pp. Striking, psychological suspense novel. ISBN 0-941483-05-3 8.95

TO THE LIGHTNING by Catherine Ennis. 208 pp. Romantic Lesbian 'Robinson Crusoe' adventure. ISBN 0-941483-06-1 8.95

THE OTHER SIDE OF VENUS by Shirley Verel. 224 pp. Luminous, romantic love story. ISBN 0-941483-07-X 8.95

DREAMS AND SWORDS by Katherine V. Forrest. 192 pp. Romantic, erotic, imaginative stories. ISBN 0-941483-03-7 8.95

MEMORY BOARD by Jane Rule. 336 pp. Memorable novel about an aging Lesbian couple. ISBN 0-941483-02-9 8.95

THE ALWAYS ANONYMOUS BEAST by Lauren Wright Douglas. 224 pp. A Caitlin Reese mystery. First in a series. ISBN 0-941483-04-5 8.95

SEARCHING FOR SPRING by Patricia A. Murphy. 224 pp. Novel about the recovery of love. ISBN 0-941483-00-2 8.95

DUSTY'S QUEEN OF HEARTS DINER by Lee Lynch. 240 pp. Romantic blue-collar novel. ISBN 0-941483-01-0 8.95

PARENTS MATTER by Ann Muller. 240 pp. Parents' relationships with Lesbian daughters and gay sons. ISBN 0-930044-91-6 9.95

THE PEARLS by Shelley Smith. 176 pp. Passion and fun in the Caribbean sun. ISBN 0-930044-93-2 7.95

MAGDALENA by Sarah Aldridge. 352 pp. Epic Lesbian novel set on three continents. ISBN 0-930044-99-1 8.95

THE BLACK AND WHITE OF IT by Ann Allen Shockley. 144 pp. Short stories. ISBN 0-930044-96-7 7.95

SAY JESUS AND COME TO ME by Ann Allen Shockley. 288 pp. Contemporary romance. ISBN 0-930044-98-3 8.95

LOVING HER by Ann Allen Shockley. 192 pp. Romantic love story. ISBN 0-930044-97-5 7.95

MURDER AT THE NIGHTWOOD BAR by Katherine V. Forrest. 240 pp. A Kate Delafield mystery. Second in a series. ISBN 0-930044-92-4 8.95

ZOE'S BOOK by Gail Pass. 224 pp. Passionate, obsessive love
story.   ISBN 0-930044-95-9   7.95

WINGED DANCER by Camarin Grae. 228 pp. Erotic Lesbian
adventure story.   ISBN 0-930044-88-6   8.95

PAZ by Camarin Grae. 336 pp. Romantic Lesbian adventurer
with the power to change the world.   ISBN 0-930044-89-4   8.95

SOUL SNATCHER by Camarin Grae. 224 pp. A puzzle, an
adventure, a mystery — Lesbian romance.   ISBN 0-930044-90-8   8.95

THE LOVE OF GOOD WOMEN by Isabel Miller. 224 pp.
Long-awaited new novel by the author of the beloved *Patience
and Sarah.*   ISBN 0-930044-81-9   8.95

THE HOUSE AT PELHAM FALLS by Brenda Weathers. 240
pp. Suspenseful Lesbian ghost story.   ISBN 0-930044-79-7   7.95

HOME IN YOUR HANDS by Lee Lynch. 240 pp. More stories
from the author of *Old Dyke Tales.*   ISBN 0-930044-80-0   7.95

EACH HAND A MAP by Anita Skeen. 112 pp. Real-life poems
that touch us all.   ISBN 0-930044-82-7   6.95

SURPLUS by Sylvia Stevenson. 342 pp. A classic early Lesbian
novel.   ISBN 0-930044-78-9   7.95

PEMBROKE PARK by Michelle Martin. 256 pp. Derring-do
and daring romance in Regency England.   ISBN 0-930044-77-0   7.95

THE LONG TRAIL by Penny Hayes. 248 pp. Vivid adventures
of two women in love in the old west.   ISBN 0-930044-76-2   8.95

HORIZON OF THE HEART by Shelley Smith. 192 pp. Hot
romance in summertime New England.   ISBN 0-930044-75-4   7.95

AN EMERGENCE OF GREEN by Katherine V. Forrest. 288
pp. Powerful novel of sexual discovery.   ISBN 0-930044-69-X   8.95

THE LESBIAN PERIODICALS INDEX edited by Claire
Potter. 432 pp. Author & subject index.   ISBN 0-930044-74-6   29.95

DESERT OF THE HEART by Jane Rule. 224 pp. A classic;
basis for the movie *Desert Hearts.*   ISBN 0-930044-73-8   7.95

SPRING FORWARD/FALL BACK by Sheila Ortiz Taylor.
288 pp. Literary novel of timeless love.   ISBN 0-930044-70-3   7.95

FOR KEEPS by Elisabeth Nonas. 144 pp. Contemporary novel
about losing and finding love.   ISBN 0-930044-71-1   7.95

TORCHLIGHT TO VALHALLA by Gale Wilhelm. 128 pp.
Classic novel by a great Lesbian writer.   ISBN 0-930044-68-1   7.95

LESBIAN NUNS: BREAKING SILENCE edited by Rosemary
Curb and Nancy Manahan. 432 pp. Unprecedented autobiographies
of religious life.   ISBN 0-930044-62-2   9.95

THE SWASHBUCKLER by Lee Lynch. 288 pp. Colorful novel
set in Greenwich Village in the sixties.   ISBN 0-930044-66-5   8.95

MISFORTUNE'S FRIEND by Sarah Aldridge. 320 pp. Historical Lesbian novel set on two continents.   ISBN 0-930044-67-3   7.95

A STUDIO OF ONE'S OWN by Ann Stokes. Edited by Dolores Klaich. 128 pp. Autobiography.   ISBN 0-930044-64-9   7.95

SEX VARIANT WOMEN IN LITERATURE by Jeannette Howard Foster. 448 pp. Literary history.   ISBN 0-930044-65-7   8.95

A HOT-EYED MODERATE by Jane Rule. 252 pp. Hard-hitting essays on gay life; writing; art.   ISBN 0-930044-57-6   7.95

INLAND PASSAGE AND OTHER STORIES by Jane Rule. 288 pp. Wide-ranging new collection.   ISBN 0-930044-56-8   7.95

WE TOO ARE DRIFTING by Gale Wilhelm. 128 pp. Timeless Lesbian novel, a masterpiece.   ISBN 0-930044-61-4   6.95

AMATEUR CITY by Katherine V. Forrest. 224 pp. A Kate Delafield mystery. First in a series.   ISBN 0-930044-55-X   7.95

THE SOPHIE HOROWITZ STORY by Sarah Schulman. 176 pp. Engaging novel of madcap intrigue.   ISBN 0-930044-54-1   7.95

THE BURNTON WIDOWS by Vickie P. McConnell. 272 pp. A Nyla Wade mystery, second in the series.   ISBN 0-930044-52-5   7.95

OLD DYKE TALES by Lee Lynch. 224 pp. Extraordinary stories of our diverse Lesbian lives.   ISBN 0-930044-51-7   8.95

DAUGHTERS OF A CORAL DAWN by Katherine V. Forrest. 240 pp. Novel set in a Lesbian new world.   ISBN 0-930044-50-9   7.95

THE PRICE OF SALT by Claire Morgan. 288 pp. A milestone novel, a beloved classic.   ISBN 0-930044-49-5   8.95

AGAINST THE SEASON by Jane Rule. 224 pp. Luminous, complex novel of interrelationships.   ISBN 0-930044-48-7   8.95

LOVERS IN THE PRESENT AFTERNOON by Kathleen Fleming. 288 pp. A novel about recovery and growth.   ISBN 0-930044-46-0   8.95

TOOTHPICK HOUSE by Lee Lynch. 264 pp. Love between two Lesbians of different classes.   ISBN 0-930044-45-2   7.95

MADAME AURORA by Sarah Aldridge. 256 pp. Historical novel featuring a charismatic "seer."   ISBN 0-930044-44-4   7.95

CURIOUS WINE by Katherine V. Forrest. 176 pp. Passionate Lesbian love story, a best-seller.   ISBN 0-930044-43-6   8.95

BLACK LESBIAN IN WHITE AMERICA by Anita Cornwell. 141 pp. Stories, essays, autobiography.   ISBN 0-930044-41-X   7.50

CONTRACT WITH THE WORLD by Jane Rule. 340 pp. Powerful, panoramic novel of gay life.   ISBN 0-930044-28-2   7.95

MRS. PORTER'S LETTER by Vicki P. McConnell. 224 pp. The first Nyla Wade mystery.   ISBN 0-930044-29-0   7.95

TO THE CLEVELAND STATION by Carol Anne Douglas.
192 pp. Interracial Lesbian love story.   ISBN 0-930044-27-4   6.95

THE NESTING PLACE by Sarah Aldridge. 224 pp. A
three-woman triangle—love conquers all!   ISBN 0-930044-26-6   7.95

THIS IS NOT FOR YOU by Jane Rule. 284 pp. A letter to a
beloved is also an intricate novel.   ISBN 0-930044-25-8   8.95

FAULTLINE by Sheila Ortiz Taylor. 140 pp. Warm, funny,
literate story of a startling family.   ISBN 0-930044-24-X   6.95

THE LESBIAN IN LITERATURE by Barbara Grier. 3d ed.
Foreword by Maida Tilchen. 240 pp. Comprehensive bibliography.
Literary ratings; rare photos.   ISBN 0-930044-23-1   7.95

ANNA'S COUNTRY by Elizabeth Lang. 208 pp. A woman
finds her Lesbian identity.   ISBN 0-930044-19-3   6.95

PRISM by Valerie Taylor. 158 pp. A love affair between two
women in their sixties.   ISBN 0-930044-18-5   6.95

BLACK LESBIANS: AN ANNOTATED BIBLIOGRAPHY
compiled by J. R. Roberts. Foreword by Barbara Smith. 112 pp.
Award-winning bibliography.   ISBN 0-930044-21-5   5.95

THE MARQUISE AND THE NOVICE by Victoria Ramstetter.
108 pp. A Lesbian Gothic novel.   ISBN 0-930044-16-9   6.95

OUTLANDER by Jane Rule. 207 pp. Short stories and essays
by one of our finest writers.   ISBN 0-930044-17-7   8.95

ALL TRUE LOVERS by Sarah Aldridge. 292 pp. Romantic
novel set in the 1930s and 1940s.   ISBN 0-930044-10-X   7.95

A WOMAN APPEARED TO ME by Renee Vivien. 65 pp. A
classic; translated by Jeannette H. Foster.   ISBN 0-930044-06-1   5.00

CYTHEREA'S BREATH by Sarah Aldridge. 240 pp. Romantic
novel about women's entrance into medicine.
  ISBN 0-930044-02-9   6.95

TOTTIE by Sarah Aldridge. 181 pp. Lesbian romance in the
turmoil of the sixties.   ISBN 0-930044-01-0   6.95

THE LATECOMER by Sarah Aldridge. 107 pp. A delicate love
story.   ISBN 0-930044-00-2   6.95

ODD GIRL OUT by Ann Bannon.   ISBN 0-930044-83-5   5.95

I AM A WOMAN by Ann Bannon.   ISBN 0-930044-84-3   5.95

WOMEN IN THE SHADOWS by Ann Bannon.
  ISBN 0-930044-85-1   5.95

JOURNEY TO A WOMAN by Ann Bannon.
  ISBN 0-930044-86-X   5.95

BEEBO BRINKER by Ann Bannon.   ISBN 0-930044-87-8   5.95
Legendary novels written in the fifties and sixties,
set in the gay mecca of Greenwich Village.

VOLUTE BOOKS

JOURNEY TO FULFILLMENT	Early classics by Valerie	3.95
A WORLD WITHOUT MEN	Taylor: The Erika Frohmann	3.95
RETURN TO LESBOS	series.	3.95

These are just a few of the many Naiad Press titles — we are the oldest and largest lesbian/feminist publishing company in the world. Please request a complete catalog. We offer personal service; we encourage and welcome direct mail orders from individuals who have limited access to bookstores carrying our publications.